AF424407

HOPELESS ROMANTICS VOL 7
Judy Finds Hans
By: Carver Wrightman

[Historical Notes:] Adolf Eichmann was hung for his Crimes Against Humanity long after WW2 was over. The details are here:
https://nypost.com/2016/01/27/eichmann-begged-israels-president-for-his-life-before-execution/

What is not generally known is that a few high-ranking Nazis were busy accepting bribes for the release of certain Concentration Camp and Holding Camp Prisoners. Enormous sums of money changed hands. The source of the funds was each freed person had loved ones with means in either North and South America paying several ransoms. (Did anyone but me ever wonder how so many ex-Nazis made it to a safe haven in a South American country during and after WW2? The travel and relocation expenses were ruinously expensive and fraught with paying bureaucratic bribes necessary along the trail?)

[About This Novel] Certain movies and novels hint that such bribery was ongoing, but was careful that the ghoulish practice never made the headlines - charitably, to keep the process going and freeing as many as possible captives from the Nazis for as long as possible. The classic example is the 1942 blockbuster, "Casablanca," where Victor Laszlo was released from a concentration camp and was on his way to America to raise more funds to free others.

Lisbon was the hotbed of ransom payments in the early stages of the war. Several German negotiators made trips to neutral Portugal to hammer out more allocations for things like foodstuffs and Tungsten . (Portugal's laudable goal as a neutral was to sell armament raw materials and foodstuffs equally to both Allies and Axis powers so they would not be invaded by either power.)

Lufthansa Condor flights from Berlin to Lisbon were common and one or two flights happened almost weekly. The negotiating teams and Nazi 'businessmen' would often travel on those flights. Often, however, a high-ranking Nazi who was ignorant of trade negotiations or business matters, 'joined' the team while lining his pockets via being secretly paid ransom money for the release of certain prisoners on the side.

This work employs some fantasy elements, in that there were **Hopeless Romantics** who found each in the scary world of Lisbon in the shadows of the bright lights. For Details of the fantasy portions, refer to the Appendix to this book.

HOPELESS ROMANTICS VOL 7
Judy Finds Hans
By: Carver Wrightman

In 1941, Hans Romberg, Highly decorated by the Fuhrer after he became a triple ace on the Eastern Front as a Luftwaffe fighter pilot, was now a Senior Pilot for Lufthansa and also a Gestapo Agent. Today on this flight he was in the process of defecting to the Allies. The means to do this was that he flew a Condor round trip on a routine from Berlin to Lisbon almost weekly.

In time the Condor airplane crossed from Germany into Vichy France on today's flight from Berlin. Hans sat in the right seat and his co-pilot was driving the airplane, while the defecting pilot handled all communication with both the passengers, the ground, and from any other aircraft encountered.

German Aircraft Control Towers kept ordering Hans to return to Berlin's Tempelhof and the senior pilot with the headphones covering his ears, simply ignored the order. The remainder of the crew was unaware of the Return Order. Hans was confident that the Messerschmidt 109's would not dare fire on the Condor in flight. The remainder of the flight crew struggled to stay awake as the weather was so calm until a coin could be stood on its edge and balanced.

After the aircraft passed over the Pyrenees into Spain, Hans began to relax ever so slightly as he felt the muscle tension gradually letting go. In a slightly upbeat mood now he switched on the coach speakers and said, "Ladies and Gentlemen, this is the co-pilot. We have just crossed over the French border with Spain and should be landing in Lisbon's Portelo Airport a half hour earlier than scheduled. The weather forecast is for a continued smooth flight until we touchdown at Lisbon and a beautiful late afternoon awaits us once we land. I have turned off the seat belt signs since air continues to be calm so enjoy the remainder of the flight. Hans's words were calming because by that time, everyone was exhausted and restless from the long flight so far. The passengers were bored out of their heads.

When the Condor entered Portugal's air space, Hans felt himself relaxing even more while noting that all radio talk coming from German sources were now silent.

Hans spoke to the Lisbon control tower on the radio on behalf of Mark, the co-pilot, who remained sitting in the left seat, driving. He had flown the plane, for the entire flight except for toilet breaks. Hans radioed, "This is Westbound Lufthansa 124 requesting permission and instructions to land."

The tower operator recited the wind direction and speed and runway number to use, and Hans relayed the information to the airplane driver and reported affirmative back to the control tower . The co-pilot sitting in the left seat flying the aircraft began to radiate pride and smiled broadly in a subtle, 'I-did-it' manner. Mark screamed to the crew as he began turning into the wind and lining up the aircraft to touchdown on the designated runway. He excitedly exclaimed to his peers, "Runway is in sight, guys. Thank you for the left-seat opportunity, Hans."

The Defector turned off the mike and felt some angst but asked his co-pilot, Mark, "Did you remind yourself we have pushed the envelope to the max and are fully loaded. You will need to touch down gently. We have a perfect day awaiting us in Lisbon. And, we must not screw it up landing. Got that?"

"Yes, Hans. "

"Then I will just be quiet and let you do it. Sweat popped out on his forehead and he said, "One last word, before I grow quiet: Don't forget to stay calm and watch for other craft and wind direction change."

"Will do." The copilot proceeded to grease the Condor onto the runway with the passengers barely feeling the wheels as they touched solid ground. The driver used most of the length of the runway to gradually slow down the aircraft and turn towards the terminal near the opposite end from touchdown.

Hans breathed deeply and he used this moment to relax completely for the first time since he talked to an informant after leaving the Adlon Hotel Bar in upscale Berlin. Romberg was now emotional with extreme happiness and his eyes turned red, though he kept his goggles over them so that it was not apparent to the other crew. For example, he was barely aware that the passengers clapped for Mark's easing the plane down then turning off onto the taxiway on the last access to the terminal.

It was Mark's first left-seat experience with an airplane loaded with people and cargo. Hearing the passengers cheering made his day.   The Junior Pilot exploded to the crew, "I wish my Mother could hear those people clapping for my first successful effort at this level!"

Clogged up in ground traffic awaiting to enter their terminal gate area to park the airplane, Hans lay back and recalled the minute events leading to this moment because his emotions were so high until he was afraid to speak.

\\\
\

The Nazi senior Gestapo agent, Adolf Eichmann, informed Hans Romberg fifteen weeks ago that the Big Shot had stepped up to the baggage claim belt in the Lisbon Portelo Airport to await his suitcase in the early Spring of 1941. At that moment in history, the Axis were winning the war.

++++++++++

Jeff Mecklenburg sat in his Boston Lab in the 21st Century watching historical events happen on his Monitors that looked back in time. He was studying the ongoing 20th Century Global

War that had started in 1914 and raged on during the first half of the 20th Century.

Eichman told him, "There was a meeting held at Adolf Hitler's Retreat, Berchtesgaden, where the topic was the logistics of moving millions of people in the occupied territories 'to the East' There were several attendees but that one who got Jeff Mecklenburg's attention was Adolf Eichmann because he would uniquely survive and escape to South America to live to be an old man. In time, however, Holocaust revenge fighters caught up with him. Jeff dispatched an AI Probe to follow this most evil war survivor, Adolf Eichmann.

++++++++++

On a Winter day in early Spring '41, Eichmann, and one, Jason Orta, an executive Pro-Nazi first vice president of an international bank headquartered in Lisbon, who were friends, greeted each other again.

Eichmann had gone to a banking conference in Sweden as security for the German legation banker's meeting and met Herr Orta. The two became fast friends lifting skirts and enjoying the nightlife of the major port city. They had remained friends ever since, and on rare occasions, Eichmann came to Lisbon on a make-work security detail accompanying some legation, but visited his banker friend and his favorite whore each time he visited.

Jason Orta, who was number two man in the bank that employed him, always showed Eichmann a good time. The bank flourished in Iberia, Germany, and Argentina and some other countries.

The two 'business' friends smiled while Eichmann did the Nazi Salute and said, "Thank you for meeting me again, Herr Orta. I am most interested in raising the kind of funds for the Third Reich alluded to in your wire. I am especially excited that you already have a good prospect with whom we might kick off this project."

The banker said, "Yes, I do. Since you and I talked, I have made progress. And it is Sunday, and no one is in my office building except bank security why don't we go to my office to discuss the new developments?"

———

Once in Orta's plush office, the two enjoyed some of the best wines in Europe. They talked about the war fronts and Orta said, "After you guys invade England, it will be smooth sailing for the Third Reich. I will wager that the Fuhrer opens a salvo against North America within a year! Both were feeling good from the effects of the wine and reinforced the conviction that the Axis would win to each other.

Orta said, "Now to business. The reason I suggested this project when we were in Sweden at the banker's meeting will become clear. Our bank has on deposit funds of an American individual customer who keeps a low seven-digits of U.S. dollars and Swiss francs balance," as he passed a folder to Eichmann. He continued, "I took the liberty of making a facsimile of all his last month's transactions for your private perusal, just to give you an idea of how he spends money and talk about his source of expenses and revenues - debits and credits."

"Wow! Who is this guy?"

"Mister Jerry Matthews wants to set up a process whereby specified Jews are released from captivity in the work and holding camps in exchange for a large amount of ransom money the Reich Treasury will enjoy - I am talking about a vast sum of money for each released person, Adolf."

There was silence in the room as the Gestapo agent sat up straight in his chair and said, "I am immensely interested, Herr Orta. You do know that our goal is to just purge undesirable people from our society, and we don't care if they travel to North America or South America or go to hell. As you well know, as an international banker, the Reich has a growing need for hard currency, and this would be an additional source of revenue. So, tell me the details."

While Orta talked, Eichmann got up and stood at the window looking down at the lighted city while listening and thinking and observed busy people walking along the sidewalks and automobile traffic on the street. He had his hands clasped behind him as if he were pondering a risky business investment. He turned around and asked, "What assurances do you suppose the representative of the American money-bags will want that we are doing our part? Also, do we have reason to believe that those 'loved ones' have the deep pockets for this kind of ongoing expense? Finally, they would want some type of guarantee that both parties will do what was agreed to bring about each person's release?"

"Herr Eichmann, I am the account executive for Mister Jerry Mathews. I know how much money he deposits, spends and what he spends it on. I know, for example, he currently spends most of his funds for bribing petty officials - and high ranking ones as well - to ransom some German, French, and Poles who are not yet incarcerated citizens out of Europe via Portugal. Bribes, Railway tickets, and intermediate hotel accommodations and food rations are among the things that run up his expenses. Matthews confided that he has a network of paid agents set up, so that they pay for exit visas and train fares and hotel accommodations in advance. You and I must set this up so that the designated Jewish prisoners will just board the airplane or train and leave for Lisbon. Matthews would be responsible for relocating the released people to either North or South America."

"What makes you think Herr Matthews would be interested continually in paying out huge sums of money for the freedom of a stream of incarcerated persons?" Eichmann turned back around and looked at the sidewalk below again.

The banker replied, "His mostly Jewish backers have deep pockets have loved ones trapped by the Reich. They are desperate to ransom prisoners for travel to Lisbon. From their point of view, it's precisely the same when , say, the mafia in Italy sometimes kidnap children of wealthy folk, and the parents pay a ransom to get them freed. Those deep-pocketed folk want their loved ones released from incarceration and brought here and then turned over to the Allies - and they can afford to pay generously for your making it happen."

Thinking out loud, Eichmann said, "Of course, Matthews is a New York attorney and makes a commission on all the money that flows through his account. You said he told you that substantially higher sums of money are available if certain people are released. Please explain that."

Orta replied, "I never solicited his business. Instead, he approached me, asking for my complicity. His words were, '... do you know of a powerful Nazi who might be interested in a deal to collect ransom for released prisoners? The funds could be money paid to the Reich treasury or a particular official as it makes no difference to my clients? Trust me. My seven digits balance will grow to eight quickly if you do. My clients have the means and will raise the money. A few successes and even more money will be raised to free even more prisoners."

Eichmann said, thinking out loud, "Of course you will get your cut, and I will incur some expenses and get my fee, but I am certain I can quietly sell this idea to my boss because of the bonanza of revenue for the Reich. Orta, where does Mister Matthews live when he is in Lisbon. I would like to meet him."

The banker was smiling big because he was already counting the money that would pass through his bank and his earnings. He said, "Mein Herr, the American is in town now and keeps a room on retainer in the Hotel Palicio, where you and your legation members are lodging, " as he handed Matthew's business card to the Reich minister showing that information.

Eichmann said, "Good. Would you inform him that I will be at the bar off the Palicio Lobby at 11:30 p.m. tomorrow late for a nightcap? I will be wearing a Green Shirt and that I would like to meet him - Ugh. Tell him he should speak of interest in the 'import opportunity' you spelled out."

There was a sense of comparative relaxation of the two thugs while Orta poured a brandy this time for Eichmann and himself. The Gestapo raised his sniffer in a toast and said, "You do good work, Herr Orta. The Thousand-Year Reich appreciates you. Now,

I need a bath and afterward relax with my Lisbon whore in my bed because I have had a long day. Will you drive me to my hotel?"

———

Monday evening in the off-lobby bar of the upscale ocean-side Palicio Casino/Hotel remained nearly empty. Most guests were at the gaming tables or sleeping, as was usual at all the casinos along the Atlantic ocean. Jerry Matthews entered the off-lobby bar about 11:15 to find himself almost alone. He ordered a beer and just waited.

The usual excitement of the hotel's guests was missing because it was late on a Monday. The Palicio was favored by the Nazis trying to spy on the Allies and vice versa. Always it had many customers milling around in the lobby outside the small bar, but the tiny bar was little more than a few stools off the main entry that everyone used as a meeting place.

———

Jerry Matthews, American Lawyer wearing a tweed suit, waited anxiously, watching the clock move toward 11:30 p.m. At that moment, a Gestapo-looking person in a green shirt swaggered in alone - he walked as if he owned the casino. The German sat down and a sexily dressed, highly made-up lady - who had followed him inside - stepped up and sat beside the man. Eichmann said in German, "Not tonight, Greta, I have a business appointment in a few minutes, and I am going to have one drink and leave - try me tomorrow night. She replied in German, "As you wish, Dear Adolf." She stood and left the bar.

Matthews stood and moved toward the new comer and said in German, "Bitte Mein Herr, are you in the import business?"

Eichmann looked at the man and stood, and even smiled. "Yes, I am. Will you bring your drink over in the light so we can see each other clearly while we talk business?"

"Surely."

Once settled, the American offered zero small talk and went

straight to the point, "I am Jerry Matthews, and on behalf of my clients, I will pay upper six even lower seven digits for certain product air shipped by you to Lisbon's Portelo Airport. Interested?"

The man listening to the New Yorker was very interested now. He looked carefully at the handsome man and asked, "Who exactly are you, and how how do you propose to handle the details of importing the merchandise?"

Jerry Matthews said, "By way of background, I am an American lawyer by education and practice but now commute between Lisbon and New York. I facilitate the exfiltration of mostly Jews from Europe - both those still free and for the first time - hopefully, now that we have met - some incarcerated ones."

Eichmann gestured, "go on."

Matthews continued, "I envision our project to be something like; I would give you a product description. Then pay you fifteen percent of the ultimate total amount of ransom we offer after receiving certain documents that show that you are doing what you said you would do. After the product lands in Lisbon in good condition and walks off the airplane on one of your Lufthansa flights, I then - and only then - pay the remaining eighty-five percent of the total ransom amount. And, I will do this in your presence along with Herr Jason Orta, banker, who says he has a close working relationship with you."

"How do I know I can trust you and that you won't embarrass the Reich by going public?"

Matthews replied, "My customers put much or in some cases all their wealth on the line for the ransoming of their loved ones. We want to get as much of this product out of Europe as possible. What possibly could be the motivation for us or them to 'go public?' Kidnapping and paying ransoms for the victim's release has been going on since we were hunter-gatherers. The quiet news will get around back home, which will prime the money pump for even increasing the hard currency amount of funds available to the Reich."

All of a sudden, Eichmann visualized himself a wealthy German living on easy street and said, "Hmm, That is true. What precisely must I do to make certain this happens and that we do not double-cross each other, Herr Lawyer?"

You must first get them released and then shuffle all the paper and grease all the palms to get this product out of Central Europe and aboard a flight to Lisbon at the Reich's expense." Matthews breathed a sigh of relief because he noted that the Nazi remained extremely interested.

Eichmann's face radiated excitement, and he asked, "How many people will know of our continuing cargo deals after it reaches the Portelo Airport - assuming good quality product reaches Lisbon?"

"Just two others - a Pan American Airways Stewardess and an off-duty PVDE agent I hired for the security of the cargo after it lands. The stewardess obtains flight and hotel reservations for the newly freed person and, spends other money on the ground for security, exit visas, permanent residence status papers in North or South America, and finally, a pre-paid clipper flight ticket out of Lisbon to New York."

Eichmann was deep in thought as giant money signs seemed to show in his eyes. He finally said, "Do you have some particular cargo already in mind?"

"Yes," as Matthews took a folded sheet of paper and a photograph out of his vest pocket and gave it to the Gestapo Agent. He continued, "Here is the photo and profile sheet and the total amount his loved ones can pay. They have listed the camp where the prisoner was last known to be held."

Eichmann looked at the surprisingly large amount of money and the location of the prisoner and said, "Hmm, Well, I am motivated, Herr Matthews. I will approach my bosses."

Jerry, hopeful now, replied, "Just to recap: you get the 15 percent when the cargo's release is certified. That means he or she holds an airline ticket to Lisbon along with exit visas from your Camp and Germany and a copy is in our hands. We will be sufficiently convinced to pay 15-percent when you send that paperwork via your banker. We ask that you send these copies via your diplomatic pouch for eventual delivery to Herr Orta. He will wire me and later give them to me. I will transfer the 15 percent if your paperwork is in order. We both know we can trust Orta because Dictator Salazar would grind him to bratwurst patties if he had a loose tongue. Once the cargo walks off the plane happy to be in Lisbon, you will get the remaining eighty-five percent."

"How will I get that?"

"The five principles involved - you, me, Orta, airline employee, and PVDE Security on private hire - will have a meeting and then - and only then - will we pay the eighty-five percent remaining. We will do our part, and you will have done yours. The mechanism is that I will sign a transfer slip of the eighty-five percent from my account to the account which Herr Orta's designates. In essence, you get the original copy, I get the second copy, and Orta gets the third copy of the money transfer. Orta will later do the appropriate bookkeeping entries at his bank."

Eichmann said, "In summary, Matthews, you pay 15 percent to motivate us to act, and then the remaining 85 percent after we five see that the Reich did act as agreed."

"Yes, succinctly stated."

Eichmann looked closely at the data-sheet and person once again and asked, "What does the giant symbol, XJ2, mean?"

Matthews, pissed off at the waste of any time, said, "That is just our project designation."

"O.K. Herr Jerry Matthews. Shall we shake hands on our agreement?"

"NO! I don't shake hands with Nazis; I just do business with them when necessary - and then only on behalf of my clients."

Both gentlemen stood, and Eichmann put the XJ2 photo and data sheet in his vest pocket as he put back on his light jacket. He said, as an afterthought, "I know that not everyone buys into the goals of our Fuhrer, so I am not offended by your discourtesy. I am impressed with you as a keen businessman concerned with details, though, and it is comforting to work with someone who knows what he is doing."

= = = = = = = = = =

The Pan American RT Lisbon/New York flights of the 314 Clippers were long and zigzagged across the Atlantic for re-provisioning and to avoid German ships and planes. Lisbon was a hated world for Brenda Smith, Intelligence Operative, and Pan Am stewardess. The layovers in Lisbon were usually three days. Aircraft frame and engine crews spent time tweaking the vessel while provisioning and maintenance were in process. Intensive inspections and preventive maintenance procedures are practiced as a safety precaution to prepare the aircraft for the 26-30 hour flight back to New York - all of which is over open water.

This Spring morning, 1941, morning, Brenda Smith, Hostess, and many friends in the crew took a long walk along the sand of the Atlantic Ocean beach adjacent to Monte Estoril Resort and Casino. Its expensive guest rooms looked out on the Atlantic, while Pan Am crew quarter rooms looked out at some scrubby woods in the rear of the hotel. The flight duty friends' goal today was to exercise by walking and beach-combing as a group and to take up or kill time and chat with of the workplace friends. Every single person dreaded tomorrow's flight to NYC and hated Lisbon.

Brenda thought, "I have another task after her exercise walk, however." She was to meet Adolf Eichmann and a local Nazi sympathizer banker, Jason Orta, along with two others at 6:30 p.m. The airline hostess-qua-intelligence agent would arrive in the private room of Pan Am's contract hotel, the Monte Estoril. It was off the main floor of the enormous buffet dining room and on the ground floor. (Those enjoying the buffet food were mostly killing time and taking a break from the gaming tables upstairs.) She grimaced and said, "I must be there promptly at 6:30 dressed to seduce as my handler ordered at least on the first meeting." Today was to be that anticipated first one.

Every flight out of and to New York had a body in every seat. Not only that, but a waiting list for each one was also two digits long and getting longer. Brenda Smith worked one of two RT flights weekly as a cabin service person. She also was the control officer of bookings to NYC from Lisbon. Brenda was in charge of rearranging flight reservations to New York when necessary. She also worked for a local Allied Intelligence senior while doing her airline job. The senior spy was allied with both the Brits and the Americans - and was Brenda's handler. Thus, her role was sometimes to allow one passenger to bump another. She did this by manipulating levels of travel authority."

Today at 6:25 P.M. Brenda Smith made her way through the giant Buffet dining room towards a small private room for a meeting. It was off the vast open area. She pondered to herself, "I wonder if I will feel like lice when I leave a meeting for the first time that was attended by two Nazis? Yuk! I miss my sailor, who is somewhere in the North Atlantic, and I miss my local hunk, who loves me as a woman wants and needs to be loved. Dealing with Nazis is not something I want to do... But, duty calls."

==========

Among the cat-calls and whistles, as the made up stunning blond made her way across the buffet dining room, a group of five Lufthansa Airlines Condor crew wearing their formal flight uniforms watched - and then screamed and whistled along with everyone. They often enjoyed the buffet dinner at the Monte Estoril because scuttlebutt was that the most beautiful women hang out there and prices were good.

All eyes were on the lady passing from the main door back to the off-room. The co-pilot said, "Hans, why don't we have engine problems so that we may return to Berlin a day later? That would give me enough time to show that lady what it is like to be bedded by a real man."

The pilot, Hans Romberg, replied, "If that were the case, I would be her obvious choice. I don't think she is looking to get laid, but she does look like she is on her way to meet someone in that private room - she has no way of knowing that here I am and not in that room?"

The five burst into laughter at the senior pilot's joke as the lady disappeared into the room, and the five returned to the serving line for deserts.

==========

Those in the private room awaiting Brenda, maintained silence. They voted earlier for her to chair the meeting. When catcalls and whistles sounded in the main dining room, everyone in the off-room drinking their highball breathed a sigh of relief that, 'It must be Brenda on her way.'

Brenda Smith graduated from High School as valedictorian and immediately was recruited by Pan Am to train to be one of their hostesses. It was her athletic ability as well as her multilingual skills that made her win over the many other candidates applying. Her hair was naturally blond, and her eyes were a deep blue, and her hard-muscled body was Greek-statute class. She had a lover whose home port was Brooklyn. He was a U.S. Navy officer on a Destroyer whose duty was somewhere on the North Atlantic. The two got together in her New York City apartment whenever they could - which wasn't often. She also had a second lover in Lisbon, who is a citizen of Portugal, Hosea Garcia. As expected, her busy love life was a secret kept from each other man in her life.

———

Miss Smith walked into the off-room, and the first person she saw was Hosea Garcia. He was a PVDE (Portugal's FBI-type police) agent. When not otherwise engaged in his official duties, the six-feet four giant official's beat was the vicinity of the Casino/Hotel Monte Estoril. He was one of three agents who kept the peace 24/7 in an environment not meant to be peaceful. His shockingly beat up face belied the gentleman he was in real life. He wore his tailored business suit like a model. He even wore a college ring. Hosea was a family man, but before he met Brenda, he also was lured into the guest rooms of a few females on their way to America. Since his first invitation to Brenda's guest room, however, his casual sexual interest in all others in the hotel ceased. At home, his wife had lost all interest in sex after their fourth child. The naturalized citizen - was born in Spain and raised in an orphanage there. His orphanage had been pillaged by the communists and he was personally repeatedly abused during the Spanish Civil War - consequently he hated all Collectivists (both Nazis and Communists).

Brenda hired him part-time to be the security specialist during the ransoming process that concerned this meeting. His job was simply to keep the peace and protect the ransomed victim as part of his duties as a paid off-duty PVDE agent.

Brenda smiled, 'Hello again,' at Jerry Matthews, the American Attorney. She nodded to both Nazis, Adolf Eichmann, and the Lisbon banker, Jason Orta. The Nazi was in Lisbon this week ostensibly as part of Albert Speer's negotiating team looking for more raw materials for the German war effort. (The Dictator of Portugal, Salazar, shipped equal quantities of food stuffs and raw materials used in armaments to both the Allies and the Axis powers.) The underlying reason Eichmann was in Lisbon and was in this room right now, however, was to receive a large sum of ransom money.

The New York attorney's presence in the meeting today was to officiate the agreed upon remaining 85 percent payment of the ransom to the Nazi. This payoff was the result of a release of a previously specified prisoner, Project XJ2.

Brenda Smith was the first to speak after she quietly closed the door. Be seated, gentlemen, and let's get this over with as soon as possible. I will talk first. She handed some paperwork to Hosea and said, "Here are the clipper tickets, exit visas, and certification documents as war refugees for two members of the XJ2 case. The freed one's spouse previously booked into the hotel at her own expense to await her husband. Also, here is the certification that the gentleman is a war refugee. There should be no glitches on their arrival in New York. Temporarily, he will be given refugee status at border control, according to the American Embassy third secretary."

She looked at the PVDE agent, "Mister Garcia, were there any glitches you wish to report when meeting the Lufthansa Condor flight at Portelo Airport?"

"No, Ma'am, it went smoothly. The victim's sponsor and I met the Condor, as instructed by Mister Matthews. The XJ2 gentleman was the last one off and was using a walking cane. The gentleman was weak from malnutrition but insisted that he walk rather than have a wheelchair brought to him. I might add that he couldn't stop crying with happiness just to be here and to see his wife standing beside me. I cleared him through Portugal's border control by using a small bribe exiting at the VIP door. I picked up his tiny suitcase and escorted the two to my car, and brought him to the Monte Estoril and escorted both to her room. I almost cried myself at the joyous reunion once they were inside their hotel room. I told them tomorrow morning's itinerary and reminded them not to open the door for anybody except me. I then said goodbye and disappeared.

"His wife will check out of the room in the morning at eight a. m. and I will be awaiting her near the check out counter."

Brenda asked, "What are your plans tomorrow?"

"I will meet them in the lobby and wait while they breakfast, and then drive them over to the Pan Am Clipper Terminal. I will wait to make sure their paperwork is stamped and approved, and they are escorted into the secure waiting room before I leave them."

Jerry Matthews stood and said, "Mister Garcia, great job, thank you. If you give me a listing of your out of pocket expenses, I will reimburse you. Also, I would like to once again thank you for helping us."

Matthews then turned to Eichmann and said, "I have already interviewed both XJ2 and his Misses. Thank you for keeping your word when I advanced you the front end 15 percent of my quoted price. I will now pay you the remaining 85 percent." Jerry wrote a figure in Swiss francs and asked Eichmann, "Is this the correct amount?"

Eichmann was visibly excited now as the Banker Orta checked

the conversion rate as the Gestapo mover and shaker looked on and licked his lips in anticipation of gaining a large chunk of Ransom money. He asked the Banker, "Jason Orta, Is the amount I calculated that will transfer from Herr Matthews account to Herr Eichmann's correct?"

"Yes, that is my figure as well. I have the account transfer form right here, if you will verify the amount, Mister Matthews, that is being transferred to the Third Reich and then sign it with two witnesses."

After Jerry signed over a high six-digit sum of Swiss Francs, Orta gave the original to the Gestapo and the second copy to Jerry Mathews and retained the third copy for his files.

Brenda stood up again and said, "I want to thank everyone for doing what they agreed to do upfront concerning the XJ2 case. May we now move on to the next Case?"

Jerry Matthews dug into his briefcase and brought out two sheets of paper, one of which had a photograph attached to it. Holding up the two pages, he said, "This is our Project ABB."

Then the Gestapo Agent Eichmann rose and said, "Before you get into that, Miss Smith, the Reich thanks each of you for doing what you agreed to do on your XJ2 case. For the future, I need to announce and request a procedure change, however. "

She nodded 'yes' and sat. The German continued, "I am going to be spending time in the East working on a special project working directly for Herr Himmler. I won't have the time to do the leg work on this project. But, I have brought a description of my assistant. I intend to bring him in on our next case. He is the chief pilot that flew the Condor here four days ago and will fly the negotiating team, including me, to Berlin tomorrow."

Then Adolf Eichmann was passing out a profile sheet on him with a photo attached. He continued, "Hans Romberg is a well trained Gestapo Agent and a former fighter pilot, and he was a triple ace on the Eastern Front. He was decorated for bravery by the Fuhrer for becoming a triple ace - but caught a piece of shrapnel in his leg and removed from flying status for the Luftwaffe. He is Gestapo, through and through, though, just like yours truly, and is a recognized senior pilot of Lufthansa flying the Condor. Do any of you have a problem with this gentleman, and will you take my word that he will act as I would have acted on this import-export matter the same as if I came? More importantly, my name will continue to appear on the forms where he will simply sign my name and initial them. The goals will not change. The Reich needs hard currency, and you represent those who want loved ones released."

Brenda stood and spoke up, "But how do we know that he has the authority with Camp Commanders and upper-echelon commanders to act on your behalf to execute this and future projects?"

"That is a fair enough question. Hans Romberg will be acting on my authority - my name will still appear on release and application documents with his initialing for me. But, again, the Pilot representing me next time is Gestapo, and he is just like me in temperament. He will do everything I would have done."

Jerry Matthews looked at Brenda and Hosea and said, "Fifteen percent front money after Mister Orta gives me the document copies is not a fortune. Mister Eichmann and his assistant understand that if no released Prisoner is walking off the specified Condor landing, then there is No Payment for the 85 percent remaining either. I think it is a reasonable risk. What do you think?"

Hosea said, "My first inclination is to say, 'If you saw the happiness on XJ2's face when I met him at the airport, just one more freed prisoner is worth the risk."

Brenda was bored now and said, "All the Nazis look the same to me. It is your clients' money at risk, so the ball is in your court, Jerry."

"I think the risk is worth it." Then Jerry Matthews gave the profile sheets of the next case, ABB, to Eichmann. He wrote the total ransom amount down offered to free ABB. We offer this amount of money for the person we want to ransom on our next case," while displaying the two sheets of paper to the Gestapo. Details include the name, the last known camp, and what she did before is all spelled out. We will pay the amount shown for the person's safe delivery to Lisbon."

Adolf Eichmann studied the documents. He finally said, "I will have my assistant in on this one and get to work on it at once. Romberg or I will communicate with you via diplomatic pouch, via Mister Orta, as usual."

Jerry turned to the banker and said, "Please have him wire me when the Gestapo's release order, German Exit Visa, and airline ticket copies arrive. I then will come into your bank when next in Lisbon to sign for the transfer of the fifteen-percent money to the Gestapo's Bank account. The eighty-five percent remaining will be paid at a future meeting just like this one."

The banker said, "Our plan works, then. You will be hearing from me, Mister Matthews."

He responded, "Thank you, Herr Orta."

The banker and Eichmann put all their paperwork away and relaxed for the first time as they stood to leave the room together. They both said, "Auf Wiedersehen," as they walked out of the small room closing the door behind them.

==========

Outside the private room, the group of five Lufthansa Flight Crew sat telling each other jokes and lying to each other about their sexual exploits when they were fighter pilots. Occasionally the buffet waitperson would come around with a decaf coffee urn to offer refills as the men were just killing time before returning to their dreaded hotel room in another hotel/casino two miles along the beach, the Palacio.

Only one person noticed that a skinny Portuguese man and Adolf Eichmann left the private room, closing the door behind them. Hans Romberg, the chief pilot, eyed his Gestapo boss but said nothing, and the others were unaware. Hans watched the two gentlemen go to the men's room and then walk out. The two Nazis were oblivious to the Lufthansa Flight Crew sitting together.

Romberg pondered silently, "Why isn't my leader conducting a meeting in our hotel? And, who could the scrawny looking man be who is buddy-buddy with my Gestapo boss? That doesn't concern me, so I will just glue my eyes on the Blond when she comes out of the room."

==========

Back in the side room, off the main dining room, Brenda Smith stood and said, "Whew! I need use the ladies and wash out my lungs after just breathing the same air that those two pieces of rancid meat breathed. How in the world can you stand to deal with those creatures, Jerry, as if you three are conducting a legitimate business operation?"

"It's like working in a packing plant, Brenda. One gets used to the philosophical smell."

Hosea chuckled and said, "Brenda, I deal with those Nazis day in and day out, and a half-hour meeting is nothing! Every once in a while, I must bang a couple of them over the head. But, it were trained to keep the scuffle from becoming a major incident - and especially an international one."

Jerry Matthews, switching from Spanish to Portuguese, said, "I am hungry after experiencing the enormous anxiety that this meeting would go well. I propose that we go to the buffet line and have our dinner with Refugees who are trying to wiggle out of this net called 'Lisbon.'"

Brenda said, "Good idea. Let's all go through the buffet line, and whoever is first, find us a table."

Later Jerry and Hosea were sitting at a table with their food in front of them. Brenda walked up, holding the hand of Hosea Garcia's best friend, Robert Wentworth. "Jerry, say hello to Mister Wentworth, Hosea's side-kick, and also my good friend and a good friend of another Pan Am Hostess who flies the first crossing each week. His accent will give him away because he sounds awfully British."

Robert Wentworth was a tall, stout, mean-looking Brit past 50 with graying hair and whose number one morning goal was to stay alive one more day. Well respected in both the British and American intelligence services, he knew, for example, and was personal friends with Wild Bill Donovan (later of OSS fame). When FDR sent his friend to England on a fact-finding mission, Wentworth met and escorted the visitor around parts of his tour. The two super spies had many things in common. For example, both were fluent in several Romance languages, and super intelligent, and nursed a vitriolic hatred of Collectivists of both stripes for starters - Nazis and Communists. [Author's note: Wentworth first appeared **Volume IV** of the **Hopeless Romantics Series**].

Robert's value to both England and the U.S., however, is that between the wars, he traveled widely in Germany selling food-stuffs to a starving populace. In that process, he learned and reported every phase of the Nazis secretly rearming themselves contrary to the 1918 Versailles disarmament treaty. (Civilization learned and responded to the facts all too late. England, France, and the US became isolationist after 1918 and would not listen to his warnings, however).

Jerry Matthews stood and shook Wentworth's hand and said, "Pleasure to meet any friend of Brenda's."

The Pan Am hostess said, "Robert and I are going to the buffet, and we will join you, but please, fellas, no shop talk and no discussion of Nazis to ruin our dinner!"

While Brenda and Wentworth were walking to the buffet line, Brenda said, "I said no shop talk, but you should know that the first case of our project 'Unlock' went off today without a glitch. The two Nazis just left us. I think our ongoing Project should experience some wide-ranging successes."

"Thank you, Brenda, because I was curious about the results of that first meeting. I spotted the two Nazis walking out the side room and then the front door. They appeared pleased with the success of the meeting as well."

==========

The four Lufthansa Crew Members were later that evening bored and tired and stuffed with food and coffee now. Mark, the co-pilot, said, "I propose let's go back to the Palicio walking along the beach - we all need the exercise."

Hans Romberg lied, "You guys go without me. I need to use the Men's Room and will go upstairs and play a few hands of draw poker and then take a taxi home using my winnings."

The navigator said, "Winnings Hell! For someone who was decorated by our Fuhrer, you play sucker odds. What makes you think you have a better chance to win here than at the Palicio?"

"Haven't you heard, I have pull with the Casino Gods."

The four chuckled and sauntered toward the front door facing the beach and disappeared. Hans Romberg raised his hand to attract a lady's attention refreshing coffee for those dining. Afterward, he returned to the desert line. He held a piece of the chocolate pie in one hand and paid the cashier in Reichsmarks with the other, tipping generously.

On his way back to his table, he made it a point to pass close to where the uncommonly beautiful blond lady sat who he had seen earlier. She was laughing and enjoying the friendship of several men at their expanded table. They all seemed enamored of her.

As Hans walked by her table, an elderly refugee to his right painfully moved her chair out in the aisle to stand using the assistance of her walker. Doing so, however, she was temporarily blocking Hans's forward movement. It gave the Lufthansa Pilot qua Gestapo officer a chance to stop and look carefully at the face of the perfectly sexy woman to his left. She caused his biochemicals to go into overdrive unlike any he had ever seen to date.

Brenda noticed him and unconsciously smiled at the man and then noticed he replied in high German to the elderly woman's apology for blocking him. The Nazi remained smiling as well, an unspoken, 'no problem.'

After hearing the German language spoken, Brenda lost interest in the man. She silently Labeled him, "Crap! Just another rancid Nazi."

Brenda took another look at the German, "That guy might be a Nazi, but he definitely appears to be one of the mythical Germanic Gods I read about in high school."

Robert Wentworth, who had been a spy since 1919, missed little and certainly did not miss the intense attraction between his star agent, Brenda, and this particular Nazi wearing a Lufthansa Pilot's uniform.

After the Nazi's passing, Brenda immediately took out a profile sheet and photo of Hans Romberg that Adolf Eichmann passed out in the meeting just ended. She handed it to Wentworth and said, "Robert, here is a profile of that German. After we finish here, I will tell you what Eichmann said about this pilot who just passed us."

The next morning at 8:45, Wentworth waited by Brenda's hotel room door for the express purpose of discussing the German Pilot-Gestapo. They would do this while walking down the stairs to the lobby for privacy. She was enroute to the Lobby to meet the 9:00 shuttle to the Pan Am Clipper Terminal. Without naming any names, Brenda described what happened in the meeting. Then she said, "That person whose picture and profile you have will substitute for Eichmann at the next meeting - he is a close associate and works for both Lufthansa as a senior pilot and as a Gestapo Agent for Eichmann. He will be acting on behalf of the senior Thug on the next ransom payoff."

Wentworth said, "Brenda, I have no way to verify this guy and what he is capable of doing because queries with the contacts I have might lead to leaking the secret of Eichmann's ransoming prisoners for personal gain. So you are at extreme risk. We must take that chance because we want to free as many people as possible."

"I know. You are telling me I am on my own dealing with this new German because mine and your conversation never happened."

"Yes, and there is one other thing. I know that my good friend, Hosea Garcia, spends some nights in your bed in the throes of passion. If that hot-blooded Latino were to suspect that you and the German have a thing going on, he will tear Mister Romberg's arms from his body and beat him over the head with them - he kills Nazis and Communists without even batting an eye when he thinks that he can get away with it. The sexual slavery ordeal he went through in a Spanish Orphanage when the Communists overran it, left an indelible mark on him. The resulting investigation of the Pilot qua Gestapo slaughter in Lisbon would be like publishing the details of our ransoming operation in the newspaper. My friend has confided in me that he has no sex-life at home - you are it, Brenda. That means that he would be passionately jealous to maintain the one he has with you."

Brenda stopped on the stairway, astounded at the consequences she now considered for the first time. "You are one smart individual, Robert, and I am glad we are on the same side in this war - I just now thought through what a liaison with the German would do to our mission. In all honesty, there was something about that Nazi that I can not explain. It got the attention of all my body chemicals. Due to the circumstances, Consider me now a block of ice to him. My instant passion for him was only a fleeting thrill between my ears."

The ultra-wise Wentworth squeezed her hand and said, "It was apparent to me that the Kraut was sexually excited as well. Keep it subdued because we just may think of some way to use both of your chemistry-driven feelings to our advantage."

Once he opened the stairwell door into the large hotel lobby, Wentworth saw his friend Hosea Garcia comfortably sitting near check out awaiting the AJ2 case released victim to show. Brenda by way of making conversation, said, "I don't get to see my best friend, Judy Becker, when I land in NY. I am dead tired, and she is getting ready to fly. But do tell her 'hello' and that she is in my thoughts."

Robert said, "Will do. Goodbye, Brenda. I promise I will tell her when she lands."

She kissed his cheek and said, "Goodbye, Robert," as she made her way toward a section of the lobby where the Pan Am Crew was assembling to await their contract shuttle bus due at 9:00 A.M.

sharp.

Robert walked over to the off-lobby coffee shop, sat, and ordered coffee and doughnuts. He observed the older refugee leaning on a cane as he and his wife approach the hotel's check out counter. Hosea Garcia joined them with a friendly greeting. He gave the two each a stringed plastic packet containing the airline tickets and all the papers they would need to exit Lisbon and for acceptance as refugees in NYC. He watched as they ceremonially put the plastic sleeves around each other's neck taking photos and laughing loudly - both were jubilantly smiling. Hosea then escorted both to his car - parked illegally at the main door - and helped the old gentleman inside. Hosea Garcia drove the three of them away directly toward Pan Am's Clipper Terminal.

When the PVDE agent returned to the Monte Estoril, he went straight to the off-lobby coffee bar and sat beside Robert Wentworth, who sat reading a newspaper. Hosea slapped his friend on his back and said, "Did you ever see a senior citizen on a walking stick dance, Robert?"

"I Can not say that I have, tell me about it!"

After the border control officer stamped their exit visas and tickets and was in the process of escorting them into the secure waiting room, they both danced with happiness. I feel good after doing what I have done, Robert, and I look forward to doing more of it."

"We both hope the same. The reality, though, is that right now, the Nazis are winning the war."

"Yeah, I know. Have some breakfast because that is all we can do for the moment."

===========

Captain Hans Romberg and the remainder of the Condor Crew rode the small chartered van toward the airport. Hans slept well enough, but he awoke this morning wondering, "Who was that woman," when visualizing Brenda?

Hans said to the driver and the others, "Let me off at the main entrance, I want to find a clean and comfortable men's room so I can shave before we are airborne."

Once inside the terminal alone, he began a search of female faces on the outside chance that she was at the airport. Then he remembered, "Dummy she flies the Clippers." Forget it, Hans, you don't have luck like that - all you get are cows with hanging flesh! There is no chance she flies into here."

"Watch where you are going, Kraut!" Hans had just bumped into a B.O.A.C. flying officer who had soap all over his face and a razor in his hand."

Hans said in his imperfect English, "Beg pardon, please excuse me," as he passed behind the man to walk down the line of stalls. Sitting in one, he said to himself sternly. "Snap out of it, and you are not sixteen years old again! You have a seven-hour flight ahead of you, where you will be in the left cockpit seat all the way. I don't have the luck that would permit me to see her again."

Later Hans was on the ground outside and walked around beneath the Condor, looking for tell-tale signs that the ground maintenance crew failed to do their jobs properly.

He walked up the stairs and into the cabin and squeezed into the left seat. The copilot, Mark, was already in the right one studying the preflight items to check before takeoff. Hans watched the copilot look at the sheet and familiarize himself and smiled confidently while Hans perused the passenger list."

For a few seconds, there was nothing to do while passengers boarded the aircraft. Freight and luggage rode up on a conveyer belt to the cargo hold. He smiled and said to himself, "I went a full ten minutes without thinking about that woman at all. Keep your mind on flying safely, Romberg!"

Later, the Condor greased onto a runway at Berlin's Tempelhof after a long but routine flight and taxied to the designated parking spot. A mobile stairway pushed to the door of the aircraft was now in place. Hans stood to thank the departing passengers for flying Lufthansa.

When Adolf Eichmann faced Hans, he said, "Nice flight, Herr pilot, especially the landing with all our heavy equipment in the hole."

"We are well below the envelope's related maximum capacity, Herr. Even so, thank you for your compliment, we appreciate you flying with us. The Gestapo boss, Eichmann, held a small advertising brochure that Hans took.

+++++++++

At that moment, the AI Probe which accompanied Eichmann 24/7, routinely duplicated itself and read the mind of several people in the airplane, and finally read Hans Romberg. The Probe immediately communicated to Jeff Mecklenburg in the 21st Century, "This person is only superficially a Nazi and Gestapo agent."

Jeff, interested now, ordered the AI Probe to stay with the Pilot 24/7."

++++++++

Riding to his Berlin apartment in a taxi later, Hans read the sales brochure Eichmann, his Gestapo boss, gave him. He cursed - it was an advertisement for a restaurant, on which Eichmann had penciled a date - tomorrow - and time to meet 8:00 P.M. He raged silently, "Bastard, Frau Susan Manfred and I were to get together in my apartment one last time before her husband returned home. "Hell! I couldn't get it up for her, anyway, because I am stuck on that Blond in Lisbon. Oh Shit! You are not sixteen years old anymore, lover boy, forget the blond!"

The next night at the dinner table in the upscale restaurant, Hans Romberg was bored. The food was not very tasty compared to what he had grown accustomed to while in Lisbon. He thought about the blond while Eichmann described his intimacy with Greta somebody, in minute detail. While Eichmann was talking nonstop, Hans thought, "I was stuck in Lisbon for a week, beachcombing, and hanging waiting for this piece-of-shit to finish his business. While the bureaucrats 'negotiated' and filled their pockets full and enjoyed some exotic wine, cigars, and upscale food. I could have spent the week in the arms of my favorite Frau, and here I am, kowtowing, to a creature from the dead. Well, I better give some feedback before Eichmann suspects that I think he is as dull as dirt."

"Did you and Greta spend lots of time on the beach working on your tans and running up and down splashing in the waves before you retired to your room?"

"Of course, and in my room she knew exactly how to get everything from a man. What did you do to kill time, Hans?"

"We, four aircrew guys, spent a lot of time beach-combing and tasting many types of exotic foods. Women? One of the guys paid some money and dipped his wick. But the women just didn't look that healthy and enticing to me."

"I saw one lady in passing, however, for whose passion I might trade my retirement pay, the rest looked like, 'rats in a cage trying to get out,' as a local columnist described refugees in Lisbon."

Eichmann replied, "Hans, they are rats in a cage, my young friend, and you did well not to dip your wick randomly."

The senior said, "Why don't I pay the bill and go to my quarters, and let's talk about the reason I am treating you to dinner?"

In front of Adolph Eichmann's quarters, they sat in his shiny BMW talking, while shining a small penlight on a piece of paper for both to see. The senior said, "If anyone anywhere within the Reich hears what I am going to say, we both are dead men on the spot, so this conversation is for four-eyes only. Are we agreed?"

Puzzled, the airplane driver who also was Gestapo and who worked directly for Eichmann, looked at his boss with a puzzled expression, "Yes sir?"

"As you know, I attended that policy meeting with the Fuhrer and Himmler in January. we are incarcerating many Jews in work camps and in the future the numbers will swell. The Reich's goal for doing this is to remove them from society while they do some work - though not enough work to justify the cost of keeping them. Well, we now use an additional method to remove certain ones from society. We use it to bring hard currency into the treasury of the Third Reich as well. You are aware that as this war rages on, we need hard currency to buy raw materials for armaments and foodstuffs, so that is why my superior and I came up with this device to raise money. Any background questions so far?"

Hans replied, "No, Sir. Your goals make sense to me. Prices are escalating, so that means there is a shortage already of consumer goods and that those that are available are going up in price - it must be happening in armaments supplies we must import as well."

"Well, Hans, I am impressed at how quickly you pick up things. But I guess you learned to fly a fighter well since you were a triple ace. But you were 'demoted' as it were to a Storch hedge hopper for hauling important people around and a senior pilot for Lufthansa because of your injury. Be that as it may, you do know I recruited you to keep an eye on those you fly to Lisbon, Madrid, or Bueno Aires."

"Well, sir, any pilot is always alert when airborne. Studying the passenger manifest a few minutes before and after each flight hasn't added that much stress."

As the clock ticked, the two Nazis dressed in their black Gestapo uniforms continued to sit in Eichmann's BMW. The senior took out the Profile Sheet and Picture of Case ABB along with a carbon copy of a letter he wrote today to a particular Gestapo Camp Commandant.

Eichmann gave the spill that he and Jason Orta discussed. Afterward, Hans used his penlight to be sure he grasped what the letter contained. It said in part, "...as part of the Jewish relocation efforts I am managing - as Reichfuhrer Himmler addressed in the general meeting in January - my assistant and I will drive over to your camp. We will arrive and interview in private Prisoner <Number>, and possibly you will discharge that person to our responsibility because we might want that person to leave the camp with us. Please have her shower and dressed in the cleanest clothes she has for the interview. We think she possibly can be more valuable to the Reich elsewhere - that is why we want to interview her privately and in person. Expect us about <time, date>…"

Hans then studied the profile of this ABB woman and asked, "May I ask why is it necessary for us to drive over to the camp?"

"Eichmann - pissed that his young subordinate would question his plan, but wanting Hans to be Gung Ho in favor of the plan - replied to him. "Possibly, we won't have to later, but right now, doing so is imperative while we set up a routine. Procedure wise, You will write and sign my name and initial future letters to the Camp Commandants. I will copy the higher-ups, but you will drive over alone and interview candidates for relocation. When I am not available - which is most of the time since I am going to be busy on this new project - , you will sign my name and initial yours. Just keep in mind, Hans, our first goal is to rid our society of these people, and to incarcerate them is just one way. This additional method is one that has the advantage that the Reich treasury swells."

"Yes! I see, Boss, and I think you have a good plan."

———

Later, after the two drove to the internment camp, the commandant said to the two Gestapo visitors, "The person you specified, is on her way here," as he laid a personnel file on the desk. I will leave and turn over her and her resident data to you. She will enter through that door," while pointing. Herr Eichmann, if you saw fit to take her with you, I desperately need the space she occupies."

While waiting, both compared the Profile sheet given by the American Lawyer in Lisbon to the one who was coming and verified it was the same person."

The young lady who entered the room had stringy hair and wore camp issued clothes, unmarked. There was no expression on her face. She looked to Hans like once upon a time she was charming and in demand by young fellas. Both Nazis just looked at her as they motioned her to have a seat. "Did you walk over here from your building, Frauline?"

"Ja."

"And how far would you say that was?"

"Almost a thousand meters."

"We will call you Anna." Hans looked at the profile sheet ABB given Eichmann in Lisbon and asked, "Who is <the name of her father> to you?"

She suddenly became vividly alive as she sat up in her chair, interested in the two men for the first time.

"He is my Father, who lives in Rhode Island."

Eichmann said, "You are leaving the camp with us right now, did you come prepared to travel in our automobile as were the Commandant's instructions?"

"Yes, sir."

"Is there anything more you would like to tell us before we go?"

"I am pregnant and have been raped by five men during the last 55 days. Right now, I trade sexual favors for the Corporal of the Guard in our building to protect me from the others and to steal better quality food for me."

Eichmann said, "We can not do anything about that, young lady, but I suggest you not tell anyone else in Germany. I will assure you that you have nothing to fear from either of us or from the people where we are taking you for temporary residence. Your next stop is a Gasthaus near the Berlin airport where you will stay until next Monday, and from there we are flying you to Lisbon, Portugal. You will be given meal tickets and left alone in the Gasthaus. Hans Romberg, here, will pick you up at 6:00 a.m. in its reception on Monday morning <date>, and fly you to Lisbon - he is the senior pilot of the flight you will be on. Your father will be awaiting you when the Condor lands in Lisbon. For this to happen, you will not breathe a word to anyone, ever, not even when you get back to America. Can you not see how important it is that this type of knowledge does not become widespread?"

The late teen was crying and said, "Yes, Sirs. You want to bring out more incarcerated people. If what you are saying happens, I promise never to speak of it, and it will be my and my father's secret. And even if all this is a lie, any other camp you take me to can not possibly be any worse than <camp>. "

Hans said, "I brought some lunch that is in the car, and you may eat it during the drive back to Berlin. - Shall we go," as he looked for confirmation from Eichmann?"

The three rose and went out of the room using the main door and entered a visitor waiting area. All three used the W.C. and calmly walked to the parking lot of the admin building and got into Eichmann's shiny BMW. The black uniforms did the trick in that all sentries waved them through as they exited the camp and drove on the autobahn back to Berlin.

Anna was beside herself with excitement as the car later approached the Gestapo-leased Gasthaus. It was near Tempelhof, aircraft engines roared, and she saw flights landing and taking off. The trio walked up to the 'hotel,' Eichmann greeted the housekeeper and introduced Hans.

The senior said, "I have another guest for you, Freda. Hans, here, will pick the guest up at six am on Monday <date>. Please <number> enough meal tickets until then and bill my office for her lodging and meals. Anyway, you can come up with a simple dress that covers the number tattooed on her arm? Bill me for that as well."

"Yes, Mein Herr, we have several for her to choose from."

Eichmann said, "Oh one other thing, "You are not going to see my smiling face so often in the future as my assistant, Hans, will be doing the leg work, but I ask that you treat a request from him as if I asked you, and continue to bill me for contracted expenses."

"And finally, Freda, she, like all the Jews you temporarily house for my department are not to be bothered by any of the other guests or your employees."

She smiled and said, "Don't worry, ReichFuhrer. They are residents isolated on the third floor, and each has a separate room, and a w.c. is at the end of the hall. The third-floor guests live apart from all the others - Staff takes food, drink, and magazines up to them and keeps the peace." She extended her hand to shake that of the young Gestapo Officer. The three of them did the Nazi salute!"

While the conversation among the thugs lasted more than a half hour, Anna could not believe what was happening to her. She sat where she was told and remained quiet as she carefully listened. She couldn't stop crying with happiness. She thought, "This is not another camp. I am leaving Germany. Oh! Could that be happening to me? I think it is, and if not, I know how to end my life."

———————

Later, Driving Hans to his quarters, Eichmann said, "Plan to spend the day in my office tomorrow. You and I will do some paper-work relative to our activities today and the first similar type activity I undertook before I brought you in on the project."

When the day was finally over, Romberg was bone tired and hungry as he trudged up three flights of stairs to his apartment. Then he remembered, "I gave my lunch to the Jew to keep her from panicking while being in the car with two Gestapo Agents. I haven't had anything to eat since breakfast. Wonder what I have in my apartment?"

His apartment door was ajar. He unsnapped his holster thinking burglars, but when he pushed the door open, he smelled bratwurst cooking. The aroma made him weak to the point that he relaxed against the wall near the door.

Frau Manfred came to the door and said, "Surprise!" She ran to her lover and embraced him while pulling out a telegram: "Engine trouble in Russia, and I will be here until a space-available seat on another flight. I will advise my ETA when known."

"The aroma of that dinner you are cooking is killing me. How soon can we eat, as I missed lunch?"

"Wash up and open a bottle of wine - the Potatoes are nearing ready."

In the W.C., Hans pressed his forehead against the mirror after washing his face and hands with soap. "Oh shit! I will be the first fighter pilot who can not get it up for her because I have yet to get the Blond in Lisbon out of my mind. If my failure to perform became public knowledge, I couldn't hold my head up among my peers on Monday. Wait! Do I care? You must perform to please Freda, Herr Romberg, because the success of your new role is essential. It is crucial both to the Reich and to the poor people we have incarcerated that we are to release."

At the dinner table, Frau Manfred and Hans chatted aimlessly. While she talked, Hans thought, "I already know more about you than I want to know, but I will listen."

Hans said, "Herr Eichmann and I drove to a worker camp today, did our business, and returned and did some follow up details."

"Oh, Sweetheart, I don't want any details as I want us to hurry up and finish eating and take me to bed. I had an exciting wet dream about you last night!"

Hans forced a smile and said, "Well, Your dream is here tonight. Let's force ourselves to clean up the kitchen before we retire for the night."

The next morning the couple almost leaned on each other because of little sleep and exhaustion. The taxi arrived, and both got inside. Frau Manfred exited at a grocery store near her Wehrmacht Officer and her home. Hans continued to the Gestapo district headquarters.

Romberg's place of work in the District Office where he went next was simply a desk in the corner of Eichmann's huge office - Two ladies worked as secretaries in the anteroom. They both smiled at the combination pilot and part-time Gestapo Agent. One said, "Guten Morgan, Hans! It's our task to entertain you if there is anything you need because Herr Eichmann is late this morning."

"Am I scheduled to fly any big-wigs in the Storch this week?"

The lead admin person came in with two flight orders for transporting a passenger this week."

Later Eichmann came in, looked at Hans, and said, "Come,

Hans, I must catch a shuttle to Poland about noon. So we must hurry and conduct our business and let me get on my way. I hope you ate and slept well last evening!"

He stuck his head out his office door and said to the primary receptionist, "No Interruptions unless Herr Himmler calls. For everyone else, I am on the road to the airport - here is my flight where they may catch me if they want to drive to Tempelhof."

Eichmann did a customary sweep of his office looking for audio devices once he locked the door to the anteroom. He then turned on the water in the lavatory in the corner of his office.

"Hans, I want to pass on some information to you that must never be discussed or even hinted. Doing so puts both of our lives at risk. Ready?"

"Yes, sir."

"Those spending their money on this project, consider paying it as ransom money for a kidnapped person. You know this is not materially different from ordinary mafia kidnappings of children in Italy that are in the news from time to time. We Aryans, however, maintain that this is our Fatherland, and the undesirables among us should not mingle in society. This alternative method you and I are using creates revenue for the Reich as well. Any questions before I detail the process by which the now incarcerated person arrives in Lisbon?"

"Nein, sir."

Eichmann looked carefully at his protege and smiled confidently. He dialed a number which he wrote on a sheet of paper along with a project number and handed it to Hans, and said to whoever was on the phone, "This is Eichmann, and this call relates to project <number>. My assistant is Gestapo Agent Romberg, who will pick up the airline ticket and the prepared exit visa for the specified person to fly from Berlin to Lisbon next Monday morning on the Condor. My assistant's name is Hans Romberg, and he will visit your office later today to pick those documents up. What would be a good time?"

"Good. Since you take lunch at your desk, look for Hans about noon, and he should be in and out. Keep in mind this project is most secret," Eichmann noted Hans writing notes to keep the process straight.

Then the senior wrote out a name and an office number and location at Tempelhof airport administration offices on the same sheet and gave it to Hans. Commit all of this to memory and burn the paper."

Romberg memorized the contents of the paper after studying it for less than a minute. He then started tearing it into piece and deposited them in an ash tray.

"Hans, the next step is to prepare a letter for the diplomatic pouch to Portugal and a copy of the airline ticket and exit visa once you pick it up at Tempelhof and make a copy. The secretary there will forward it over to our banker, Jason Orta. Herr Orta will then contact the person paying for this service, who will transfer fifteen percent of this total to our project account - which is in my account for the time being."

Hans did the mental arithmetic and noted that this total amount would be more significant than the previous.

Eichmann looked at the knowledgeable officer and asked, "Any questions, so far?"

"Nein."

"Herr Orta will contact you at the Palacio to tell you of a meeting which happens during your layover there. Your responsibility is to exactly do what he says and don't even hint that you know this money is going to anybody - you're just a classified message carrier. if you are a religious person, Hans, don't even tell your confessor."

Hans snickered. "I will try not to, ReichFuhrer." Even Eichmann grinned.

"Finally, your other responsibility is to a meeting in Lisbon to be certain this amount in American or Swiss currency are transferred to this account number in your presence," pointing at the account number, "and after done so, and signed by the American lawyer, Jerry Matthews. Our banker will give the top copy of the fund's transfer to you. The second copy goes to the American Lawyer, and Orta keeps the third for the bank's bookkeeping purposes.

"Once the money is safely in the Reich's account, the final step is that he will give you a profile sheet and photo of the next subject he wants to ransom. You will bring that back to Berlin along with the top copy of the money transfer form back with you - again, lose it in all your navigation documents at home as a means of maximum security. I should be back in time to work with you on releasing our next person from one of the camps - if not, you know the process."

"Got all of that?"

"Yes, sir."

"Recite all the steps back to me."

After Hans spoke the steps backwards and forward as if he were stating his name and address, Eichmann stood up, causing the junior officer to stand. Hans started writing the Camp commander and signing for Herr Eichmann.

"You are super intelligent, just as informed when I recruited you. Thank you, and the Third Reich thanks you. Now for the security matters."

"I can not impress upon you too much that any paper trail you leave, must not be found. File them among airplane, engine, and navigation paraphernalia. I remember seeing you have several volumes on flying loose leaf text books. Any curious or even suspicious co-worker who searches that stuff will just pass right over it without connecting the dots. If someone were to search your apartment tonight, for example, the airline ticket and exit visa you will pick up at noon must be lost among all the airplane and airport specifications you carry with you."

Hans asked, "Why not just file them in your wall safe, Reichfuhrer?"

"Good question. But, I have some most secret documents in my safe, for my eyes only. Herr Himmler ordered me not to give you or anyone else the combination to my safe."

"Will I be reimbursed for out of pocket expenses like parking, etc.?"

Relaxed and confident now, Eichmann said, "Yes, we expect

you to incur some expenses, and among those are extra pay for you and me," as the chief said with a naughty smile.

Hans felt a slightly nauseous feeling at the top of his stomach because of what he heard. He imagined Italian Mafia gangsters in a kidnapping operation. But, he stood and said, "I am excited. With the kind of money they are talking about, wouldn't it be nice if all my flights to Lisbon were moneymakers?"

Eichmann stood now, turned off the running water. "It would be wonderful, but even rich and powerful, North and South American Jews don't have that much money!"

Eichmann went to his wall safe and said, "Stand by, and you can drive me to Tempelhof and keep my car at your quarters over the weekend. Monday morning, please leave it in the VIP lot at Tempelhof after you pick up the freed girl at the Gasthaus. I will return from Poland later that day, I will locate and drive my car home using my duplicate key."

==========

It was a long week for Hans as he flew at least one and some-times two bureaucrats in the Storch (think Piper Cub on steroids) in his regular job at the Gestapo. Passengers complimented Hans on his ability to land and take off the tiny aircraft in tight places. Sometimes the passenger bureaucrats would treat the pilot as a glorified taxi driver and talk evasively about his particular pro-ject - a recurring complaint falling on deaf ears was, "I am just one man, how can I do all that?"

When Friday night rolled around, Mrs. Manfred wrote Hans a wire, "Whole weekend tied up with family matters. Sorry."

That meant that Hans did what he hated doing the most - visited the Adlon Hotel bar to hang out. Many of Berlin's most beautiful women came to woo the flyers and pretend to be inter-ested in them - and vice versa. His favorite fun, however, was talking about flying when he often would meet another airplane driver at the bar. His libido was pegging zero because of the stress of being both a Gestapo agent and a senior pilot for Lufthansa.

Hans felt glad that Mrs. Manfred and he could not share intimacies because the blond in Lisbon remained in the back of his mind.

Tonight at the bar every time a voluptuous Frauline would smile at him - which was often - because he wore his Lufthansa Senior Pilot Uniform - the blonde lady in Lisbon popped into his mind.   Hans quickly lost interest in casual sex at any rate. In the past, Mrs. Manfred's husband was stranded in Russia so often, until she just wore out her welcome in his apartment. During that time, when occasionally alone in places like the Adlon Hotel bar, Hans walked around drained of genital body fluids most of the time. But, he loved the environment in one sense because, more often than not, he talked flying with other pilots.

This Saturday night, he renewed his acquaintance with a Lufthansa Condor driver, who flew weekly to Buena Aires. Hans asked, "William, right?"

"Ja. My friends call me Willi!"

Hans said, "Hmm, I heard the streets in Argentina are gold, and every woman there is gorgeous and wants to dance you to her bed. Is that true?"

Willi looked at him and grinned, "There is some truth in what you say - a tiny bit. Seriously, my layovers are long there, and the locals have taught me the finer points of dancing the Tango and... other things," as he casually took a sip of some expensive schnapps.

Hans returned his smile and said, "Tell me about dancing."

"Well, the women who will talk to a German pilot love to dance. They do that in a pub like this, rather than just sit around and drink as our ladies do. Then maybe you wind up going to bed with one, but I stay away from the commercials. Argentines, as they are, by and large, deeply religious and are reluctant to accommodate the sexual desires of an airplane driver."

Hans asked, "Hmm, that doesn't sound so good, so do you have to fly back here to get laid?"

"Well, lately no, but in the norm, yes - unless I want to go the pay upfront route. What is your beat nowadays, Hans?"

"Berlin to Lisbon and back - and occasionally twice in one

week, and sometimes I just hang out and wait while bureaucrats are attending meetings for the war effort."

Willi Shoemaker replied, "I stop at Portelo for maintenance, provisioning, and refueling, but my knowledge of Lisbon is limited to the Pilots Lounge only in the airport. I take a nap while I wait for servicing of my craft."

"Well, by and large, the Refugees in Lisbon are underfed, nervous, anxiety-ridden, and all that implies. The only goal they have is to leave Lisbon - although they are glad to be there as opposed to places where National Socialism reigns. They enjoy the abundance of good food and drink, unlike the rest of Europe. The lights are on at night, and live bands entertain in many saloons. The waiting to leave process for them is long and frustrating. Moreover, the lady folk have zero interest in the things an airplane driver wants. The local ladies, too, are very religious and not very interested in Germans or Brits or Americans - in that order - for a roll in the hay, especially we Germans."

William continued after a pause, "I would trade routes because we fly many, many miles over the water with no nearby landmass."

"Oh, I didn't think about that. If you lost one engine forward progress is slowed but possible, but two engines would mean you are going sit down in the water - and become targets of Allied submarines, right?"

Willi said, "And in this new era of taking no prisoners, well, its goodbye cruel world should that happen!"

"Thank goodness I am not the driver on your route."

Williams said, "Changing the subject, I think that the Argentines have the best heavy beef dinners in the world and the best coffee and wine to go along with their meals and beautiful women for sale - all of it unbelievably cheap. Food wise, returning to Berlin is a bummer."

The two continued talking airplanes and flying for two hours, neither of them tipsy. They finally said their goodbyes. Hans felt good because he had not over drank and didn't feel like he had wasted an evening.

Back in his quarters, Hans lay in bed, unable to sleep. He had forgotten entirely what he and William had talked about and just stared at the ceiling and thought about the blond-haired woman in Lisbon."

Monday morning at ten minutes until 6:00 a.m., Hans walked into the Gestapo-rented Gasthaus. There were two older ladies and one very young one who were awaiting someone to pick them up. Both the older ladies were frightened of Romberg's black uniform, but not the younger one. She could not suppress a quick smile as a cheer after seeing the visitor. Hans had to paste his ugliest grimace on his face to keep from smiling back at her. But, neither spoke in a kind of greeting.

In the typical Nazi way, which he learned in his training, Hans growled, "Grab your bag and come with me!" The two left the waiting room and went to the registration desk, where a clerk said nothing but forwarded a clipboard with a log sheet which Hans filled out and signed Adolf Eichmann's name and wrote his initials above it. He then noted the time the guest departed."

The lady, Anna, opened the back door of his BMW and entered the vehicle, and the two drove in silence in the early morning traffic. As the BMW approached Tempelhof, the young lady started crying.

He said plaintively "Here, don't cry because I don't want anyone to think I personally mistreated you." Once the horizontal steel bar to the VIP parking lot at Tempelhof went up, and the BMW sped into the now nearly empty garage, he parked near the stairway leading to the gates. Hans fetched his suitcase from the trunk and turned to her to give her a sealed plastic sleeve containing a sheet of paper with Swastikas on it. He said, "This is your airline ticket. This sleeve contains your exit visa from Germany, and you will note the Gestapo sealed it. Keep it in the clear plastic sleeve around your neck when you present it and your ticket for a boarding pass - don't worry, no one will dare question it." He gave her twenty Reichsmarks from his pocket and said, buy some food and drink and sit in the waiting room until boarding time since you missed breakfast at the Gasthaus. Keep in mind that you are a subject of the Reich until the airplane touches down at Lisbon's Portelo Airport. That means you are not a free person yet. Finally, Anna, my paperwork indicates someone you know, and love will meet you in Lisbon. Oh! One final thing. You already know I am the pilot of the airplane that will take you to Lisbon. Don't act as if you have ever seen me should we meet aboard the craft. You should begin boarding in about an hour. Any problems with my instructions, and are there any questions?"

Still too overwhelmed to talk, Anna shook her head "no' and mouthed "Thank you," in German.

There was an arrow pointing to a flight of stairs through a door that read, "To all gates." The young lady, who Hans remembered her name was Anna, disappeared up the stairs.

Later, when flying, the weather patterns worsened, and the turbulence was so severe until the Condor's cabin service crew had to take their seat and could not serve drinks or food at first. Once they finally crossed over the Pyrenees, the weather calmed, and the staff did manage to resume drink service and then began the delayed lunch service.

Anna's boarding pass assigned her to the rear seat, where she sat alone. She ignored the turbulence, while some others were screaming. Some men were even praying at the height of it. Anna's circling thoughts were, "Well, I have only myself to blame - I stayed in Grenoble after the winter because I thought I was in love with my ski instructor, and the Nazis came by early summer, they sent all foreign students to a Paris-bound Train, except we four Jews. We could not leave and had to stay there in the dorm for almost a year. They didn't know what to do with us at first. Then they finally shipped us off to camps."

In the cockpit, Hans calmly did all that a reliable professional would do. Mark, the co-pilot, said, "If we were to arc south a couple of hundred miles, the flight would be drastically late, but the passengers would feel better."

"I considered that, but one of our passengers has a date with destiny in Lisbon, and we need to arrive very close to on time."

"Oh! I figured it was something like that."

The passengers loudly cheered when finally they felt the wheels touch the runway at Lisbon.

After chocking the wheels near the terminal gate, the co-pilot helped the cabin staff clean the galley caused by the violent wind currents. The storm caused an enormous mess because of spilled drinks and broken dishes. Hans stood alone in the cockpit and smiled at each departing passenger. "Thanks for flying with us, and sorry about the turbulence."

The last passenger to exit was Anna, and he made the same speech to her that he had been giving the others. But, the young, freed woman only smiled at him and said, "Thank you for bringing me here. I owe you my life," as she stepped out the main door onto the portable stairs rolled up to the airplane.

+++++++++

The AI Probe from the future following Romberg, duplicated itself and checked the mindset of a number of passengers. When it read Anna's, it noted that the two **HOPELESS ROMANTICS** had found each other and communicated the news to Jeff Mecklenburg in the 21st Century.

Jeff examined the the two mind contents and concluded, "Neither are in a position to see the ideal person in the other yet, but that will come." He ordered her Probe to follow her 24/7.,

++++++++++

Once in the terminal, Anna saw her father standing beside a huge and stout, but well dressed dark-skin Portuguese man. - The parent and offspring raced toward each other for their reunion. The older man looked at his daughter and kept wiping his tears as both were overwrought with happiness. After Mister Bass introduced Anna to Hosea Garcia, an off-duty PVDE police officer on private hire, the dark man offered to take her one small bag she brought with her. Hosea's kindness was shocking to her. The three went directly to the VIP airport exit, where Hosea 'tipped' the sentry on duty, and the three went to the parking lot and loaded into his car.

Mister Bass, Anna's father, asked, "Are either of you hungry?"

His daughter said, "No, Dad, I am not. Lufthansa didn't feed us until we crossed into Spain because of very rough weather over Germany and France, so I just recently finished eating."

Hosea said, Mister Bass, there is a splendid buffet in the Monte Estoril where you are staying, and they open precisely at 5:30. I would suggest one gets value for one's money there."

"Dad, that sounds like more in line with what I want. I have been eating damned Kraut-food for six days held up in a Gasthaus after being released from the camp. But that was much better than the rations we got at the camp. I would love to have a fresh deep-sea fish dinner."

"That is their specialty, Anna, and the executive chef was the Pride of Paris Cuisine before the German's invaded France."

Anna smiled and corrected Hosea's English, and, "Then, if you can wait, Dad, how about a fish dinner?"

"Anything for you, Pumpkin!"

As they pulled into the circular driveway of the Monte Estoril hotel, Hosea said, "The role I play is that I am in charge of your security until you are processed out of Portugal and are awaiting your clipper flight in their secured waiting room. Your flight happens in three days. I am going to ask that if you go to the beach or shopping, you invite me along - you must understand that there are many people in Lisbon trying to leave for North or South America, so that means we live in a dangerous city."

"I understand, Dear Sir, and so just think of me as a pet with you holding the leash." Hosea didn't get the humorous metaphor at first, but then his whole face lit up with laughter when he figured it out.

At that moment, Anna thought, "When that guy is fully alive, it is like experiencing one of those Aha Moments. He is brutally ugly in a way that he is handsome in one sense.   That makes him cute and attractive. Don't even think about a man, but think about what to do with this baby you are carrying fathered by a brain-dead Nazi monster guard. Wait! Hosea probably knows a doctor."

Once in the lobby of the hotel, Jerry Matthews recognized Hosea and, by extension, the young lady and her father with him. He thought, "She must be ABB case, and the fifty-something man must be her father. He walked up to her security and said, "Hosea, nice to see you. Who are your friends?"

The security guard said, "Mister Matthews, meet Mister Bass and his daughter Anna Bass who came in from Berlin on the Condor flight today."

He turned to Anna and said, "Let me be first to "Congratulate you on your escape from the Third Reich, Anna. Once you were in our hands, did anything happen that made you feel unsafe?"

"Oh, no, Sir! Everything just seemed to work right on schedule."

Your father and now I must impress upon you to fabricate a story of how you got out of Germany. You met and seduced a Gestapo officer who ferreted you out of the camp and out of the country. The reason we ask you to lie is that we don't want the real procedure of ransoming prisoners to be widely known."

"Of course, you want to rescue others. Yes, you have my word, Mister Matthews."

Jerry relaxed and said, "If Hosea and I may accompany you two to your room, we will say goodbye afterward."

Once inside the hotel room, Hosea went through his trained procedures to look for any kind of listening device. He was satisfied that none were there. Jerry Matthews' only reason for coming was that he wanted to see the young girl healthy enough to climb the stairs and enter her room. This was for the recorded billable hours to the client.

Just as the gentlemen were leaving, Anna said, "Hosea, I want to splash in the ocean water. What time do you get to the hotel tomorrow, and could you come a little early to accompany me?"

"My shift in the gaming rooms mostly is from 3 pm to 3 am,

but part time employer pays me to be with you when you leave this room - which I will explain in the afternoon - say, would one o'clock work?"

She held his hand and said, "Oh, thank you. That will give Dad and me time to get to know each other again - and Dad chooses to stay as far away from the beach as possible - even though he made a fortune custom building yachts and sailing craft."

==========

Anna and Hosea sat on a towel in an area where people were sparse. He said, "More on what I was talking about yesterday, "The Socialists - especially those who call themselves Nazis - and Communists - have lots of enemies in their ranks. That means that those Collectivists have people watching them all the time. That means that if they should find out that we are ransoming prisoners, then all of those Nazis we depend on to make this ransoming happen will go public just to disgrace the people who work with us. Stick to the lie that I told you earlier. Everybody can believe that. Does that make sense?"

"Thank you for filling in the details." She paused thinking how she would couch her next request. "I will. Now I have something personal and private to ask you. May I, Hosea?"

"Of course."

"I am pregnant with a Nazi guard's baby - I was used repeatedly by the corporal of the guard of our barracks in the camp. I allowed him to use me because he kept the others away from me and brought better food than what was generally available to the others."

Hosea was shocked and seething with hatred inside himself and he grimaced remembering how the Communist forces abused him at his orphanage during the civil war in Spain. Hosea just looked at her and felt contempt for men who would do something like that as two tears rolled down the giant's face.

She continued, "I told Dad of my situation last night and that I want to have the baby aborted. He was shocked but reluctantly agreed. So I took it upon myself to ask if you knew of a surgeon and a clinic who performs these operations?"

"I don't know of one, but I do know some clinics secretly practice that, and I know several people who have contacts in all areas of society - it will cost your father even more money after all he spent so much to ransom you."

"Hosea, it is my money, he was and will be spending, not my father's. Will you make some inquiries and get back to me? I have the means to stay in Lisbon for a while if that is required."

"Absolutely."

After Hosea escorted Anna Bass back to her hotel room door, she squeezed his hand as a 'thank you' gesture. He walked down the stairs to the gaming rooms and walked around the sparsely packed gambling main area. Many gaming table employees sat awaiting customers, and he periodically stopped to chat with those who had grown to be friends with since '38. In particular, a Frenchman croupier formerly from the Nice area and Hosea had become close friends. Today, Hosea walked up to him and asked, "When is your next break, Ramon?"

"Anytime, good buddy - those now invisible players lined up to get to the roulette wheel will become visible later. The two walked in the employee break room that was also empty, and the PVDE agent fetched two glasses of water and sat across from Ramon." The croupier waited to see what was on his good friend's mind.

Hosea finally said, "You guys don't have much to do before the afternoon, do you?"

"No, we don't - but we didn't come here to talk about Monte Estoril's gaming business, Hosea. What is on your mind?"

"No." The PVDE agent took one last look around to confirm they were still alone and said, "I know a 19-year-old girl who is about one to two - months pregnant because she was repeatedly raped by Nazi guards when incarcerated in Germany. The refugee wants an abortion. This person has the means so that she does not have to go to a back-alley practitioner. She searches for and can pay well to have the procedure done in a germ free clinic. It must be in a sanitized operating room where the doctor and his help are professionals. Do you know a surgeon who can and will help - there is a five hundred American Dollars finders fee in it for you?"

Very interested now, Ramon sat up straight. "That is practiced here in the shadows because this is a Catholic country. Many French ladies make their way here who were raped by the Wehrmacht soldiers and find themselves pregnant. The usual procedure is to remove the fetus and show the paperwork as something else. Sutures are sometimes placed on the victim's skin as if they removed a growth. Their pretensions show on hospital and doctor's records as 'possibly malignant growth.'"

"Wow! If you deal with such a specialist, will you have him contact me in the evening as quickly as possible - tell him to comment on 'how nice Grenoble was before the Nazis.' I will be in the building after three P.M. daily - and here are two hundred and fifty U. S. Dollars to motivate you to search and keep this secret. You get the remaining 250 after the patient leaves the clinic."

Excited now, the croupier said, "O.K., my good friend, Hosea. Ask the young lady to stand by and a doctor will identify himself to you. From there, you introduce the doctor to the girl.

———————

The next evening after the Buffet had just opened in the Monte Estoril, and the Pan Am stewardess from the first flight each week, Judy Becker, sat with the British Agent, who was Judy's sperm-donor father, Robert Wentworth, and her best Portuguese friend, Hosea Garcia. (To learn about Judy, see **Volume IV** of **Hopeless Romantics**) Robert Wentworth was all aglow because every time Judy flew, he was on pins and needles. Here she was today psyching herself up to make the 30-36 hour flight to NY city in the morning. Tonight was the first time that she had a chance to visit with her sperm-donor father this trip.

Wentworth's first question was, "How is the love of your life, Judy?"

"Well, Dad, Jacque is still riding the train to the aircraft factory where he builds wooden boxes for parts." They drank coffee while it was still too early to be hungry and visited - as much as both wanted to; however, they did not hold hands for security reasons. The two rose and Robert walked her up the stairs to her room door. She looked around to find the hall vacant and hugged each other good night after they talked about her mother, Robert's wife, still in England.

"Oh, Robert, " as she squeezed his hand, lovingly, "I do understand, and someday I will call you 'Dad' openly. Right now, we both must work to win the war."

———

Robert Wentworth sat down with Hosea, and they began discussing today's work in hushed tones. A half-hour later, a well-dressed gentleman, who carried a small suitcase, and a lady came up to their table. The gentleman asked the Duo, "Mister Hosea Garcia?"

Hosea stood, and said, "At your service."

"May we talk to you in private?"

"Robert, it looks like PVDE business. Please excuse me."

The trio walked away from the table to a darkened area not yet filled by people, and said to the stranger and his companion, "Why did you want to see me, Mister?"

The man put a business card in his hand and said, "Grenoble was wonderful until the Germans came!"

Hosea smiled, extended his hand in a shake, and introduced himself, and the doctor said, "This is my nurse, who is my sister, Ruth. I practice at the <named hospital>, and in our small clinic in my home where I normally see non-surgery patients."

Hosea said, please sit down and wait for me, as I shall return in just a few moments. He sprinted up the stairs to Mister Bass and Anna's room door and knocked.

"Who is it?"

"It's Hosea Garcia, may I come in for a moment?"

The chains came off, and the door opened to reveal a smiling Anna Bass and her somber father standing right behind her. The gentleman was obviously ready to fly in the morning. After Hosea was inside and the door was closed, he gave them both calling cards and an advertisement for a clinic and a major hospital. He said, "The doctor and his nurse are downstairs, and he wants to come up and examine you, Anna. May I escort the two up right now?"

Anna looked at her father, who was non-committal and said, "Please, do so as this is the perfect time."

Later the Doctor, nurse, and Hosea were back, and they opened the door wide for them to enter. The physician opened his bag and got right to business without small talk. He said, "I need to examine your vitals, and then we will proceed from there. Mister Garcia, will you please remain in the W.C. to give privacy to Miss Anna. Young lady, please take your gown off but not your under-clothes. Then have a seat on the bed."

The doctor took out the stethoscope and began listening to her heart and lungs, he looked into her mouth and eyes and ears and said, "Lie down on your back and try to relax as much as you can. He then placed the stethoscope beneath her underwear and listened to the faint beat of the fetus's heart. He asked about her last menstrual cycle and finally asked, "Do you have any pain or nausea?"

"No, Sir."

"You may put on your gown and Mister Bass, if you would, ask the gentleman in the W.C. to join us. Anna, you are pregnant but no more than seven weeks. I have performed 16 of these abortion procedures so far, and you are at the limit of where the proced-ure will be routine. You can think the lucky stars that you remain physically fit though I see a Nazi tattoo on your arm. Since your muscles tell me you were once a world-class athlete, your recov-ery will be of short duration. He smiled and said, "Speaking of skiing Grenoble, was your preference skiing, downhill or a cross country?"

Anna smiled at the man suddenly relating to a kindred soul and said, "Cross Country, mostly, but downhill sometimes as well. I take it you have skied there. Thank you for asking."

"Yes, I have. Lucky you for getting out of the Gestapo Death Chamber when you did. When are you scheduled to fly to New York?"

Hosea interrupted and said, "It was tomorrow's flight, but I can have her trip to NYC postponed."

The surgeon looked at both the patient and her father and back to Hosea and said, "Anna, I recommend you postpone that for at least two weeks to be sure you have completely healed. Thirty-plus hours crossing the Atlantic after six days might not be wise."

The doctor emerged from the bathroom drying his hands and said, " At any rate, my official diagnosis and the hospital records will show - if asked - you had a growth on your lower abdomen that appears to be cancerous, and that we removed it early as a standard procedure to save your life. Got that?"

"Yes, sir."

"We can do this as early as tomorrow evening, and the hospital is a short cab ride from here. My nurse will return you to your room after the procedure is finished." He stated a turn-key cost payable in advance. I am available to meet you at American Express or any bank that caters to the Americans tomorrow. Call me at this number, state where and when I can meet you after you have talked this over with each other and have the funds available. Finally, we ask that whatever you decide to do, my examination and our conversation never happened. Agreed?"

Both Mister Bass and Anna said, "Yes."

The doctor and his nurse quietly left the room.

The PVDE agent stood inside the room door about to leave when Anna came up and hugged his neck, "Oh, Thank you, Hosea. Here is the one thousand dollars I promised you as a finder's fee. What a marvelous gentleman you are!"

When Anna was alone with her Dad, he said, "You do know,

young lady, you are spending your trust fund money like there is no tomorrow, and if Hitler or Stalin wins this war, you just might wish you would have spent it more quickly than you are doing!"

Anna hugged her Dad and said, "Thanks for your support, Dad. But, the maintenance of a free, industrial society is what this war against the axis means. Tribal leader thugs like Hitler and Tojo and Stalin don't have a chance. Another example of why we will win this war is that those people who freed me and who will attend to me medically did so to line their pockets. People do amazing things when paid well to do them in a free society."

"Yeah, I know that, and it's what I counted on upfront when Mister Matthews first wrote me and explained what he might do for us. I am proud of you, Anna for doing what it takes to survive and fight the evil turned loose on the world."

==========

Hans Romberg spent the day on the beach behind the Palacio Resort with his air crew friends. Most of the sun worshipers were German or Northern European people trying to find the sun. Their white skin generally showed signs of a poor diet before they got to Lisbon. The consensus of the four-person crew who were there in the sunny but somewhat chilly air was, "Mark, the co-pilot, said, "Few women here are worth looking at - someone should tell'em to keep their clothes on!"

The others chuckled, and finally, Hans said, "You guys must try to get along without me. I intend to get laid on this trip, and that is not a group effort!"

The co-pilot said, "What the hell! I thought you had a lady in Berlin who took care of your needs." Another spoke and said, "I heard it was a traveling Wehrmacht Husband's lady."

Hans lied, "You guys are crazy, I go down to the Adlon and sometimes get laid - but at a staggering cost for drinks and food."

Another spoke up and said, "You would be smart, Hans, if you paid upfront and didn't try to seduce any of those Broads."

Hans replied, "The prize goes to the only smart one of you

bunch of aviators, but I sure would like to sword fight where both the lady and I got a reward for our effort. At any rate, I am looking for something better than what I have known, so don't be surprised if I don't want to go out with you guys. When the master swordsman works, he needs privacy." Everyone said in unison, "Like hell, you say."

The quartet broke up and went their separate ways. Jason had a front-desk message stuffed under Hans's door that said, "I will pick you up at 6:00 P.M. on <date> for a meeting. Jason O."

The next evening, Hans was watching cars pull into the circular driveway of the Palacio. He stood wearing a summer-weight suit and had even shined his shoes to a bright luster - as he often did when a fighter pilot. A car pulled up and lowered the passenger side window and said, "Greetings, Herr Romberg. Get in, if you would please, sir. I am Jason Orta, and a mutual friend said we should get together."

Hans remembered the name and said, "Guten Tag, Herr Orta," as he opened the car door and jumped inside.

Orta continued, "You look like a successful businessman for sure. This meeting we will attend will only last a half-hour or so. I presume the cargo you brought back from Berlin was in good health and glad to be here, and walked off the airplane, is that right?"

"Yes, Sir. The whole process was uneventful, except there was some severe turbulence over France."

"Haha. I heard about that, as one of my clients was on your flight and said, he couldn't even buy Schnapps en route the air was so rough. About tonight, let me do most of the talking while you just smile and be your handsome self and agree if you would. If something happens that you don't understand, ask me after the short meeting."

Hans replied, "I understand. The best way to learn something is to stop talking so much - so said, my mother."

Once the two made their way to the now-empty private room inside the Monte Estoril just off the buffet dining floor, both took a seat, and Orta took out several papers from his briefcase. The banker said, "While we are alone, lets…"

Hans put his finger to his lips and said, "Shhhhh" He jumped up on the table and finding nothing in the light fixture. He then quickly took the faceplate off the light switch and replaced it. "Sorry, now go ahead."

"Wow! You have a presence of mind of a clandestine agent, thank you. Your boss did not use such precautions. As I was saying, your only two tasks tonight are to sign Herr Eichmann's name and initial your HR as signing for him. I have a copy of your initials on the identification file. The second thing is that a profile sheet of the next cargo containing a snapshot will be presented. And you will study and it, and then you already know the procedure after you return to Germany tomorrow. Right?"

"Yes, Herr Eichmann made me recite it backward and forward."

"Well, he did say you are among the brightest lights in the Third Reich."

Just then, the next party to enter the room was the American Lawyer, Jerry Matthews. Both Nazis stood, while Hans snapped his heels together after Orta introduced them. There were no handshakes offered. Matthews sat down on the opposite side of Orta and began looking through the papers in his briefcase. The three silently waited until the very tall and stout Native Iberian walked in, and circled around the table. Matthews said, "Herr Romberg, this is Hosea Garcia, a local, and Mister Garcia keeps the Peace in the Monte Estoril and nearby as a member of the PVDE. Contact him should you need the services of the Portugal State Police. His part-time job, however, is that he works for us doing security details. That way, Hosea can afford to feed his four children at home."

There was a small laugher, but then that was followed by silence.

After about three minutes, cat-calls and whistling coming

from the giant buffet dining room sounded, which by this time was half-full of people. Hans already knew the blond was coming to the small room from previous experience, but he once again criticized himself, "If you pursue her, Mister Sword-fighter, your life is at risk!"

When the lady entered the room, the four gentlemen stood, and Jason Orta said, "Frauline Brenda Smith, this gentleman is Hans Romberg, the substitute who Herr Eichmann alluded to in our last meeting." There was no handshake or touch, but inexplicably, she wanted to touch the man and thought, "Don't even think it, Brenda!"

Seeing her occasional secret lover , Hosea, and then looking over at Hans Romberg, her first thought was, "Wow! Wentworth was right! Hosea would tear off Romberg's arms and beat him over the head with them if the Kraut became my lover. Stick to business, and you might come out of this war alive." So, Brenda kept a straight face, and their meeting was underway.

Once the reporting, signing and initialing had taken place, Jerry Matthews handed the profile and picture of the next Cargo to Import to Hans. The considerable sum of money to be paid out listed at the top of the profile sheet jumped out at the surprised Gestapo Agent qua Lufthansa Pilot. He put that in his briefcase and took a seat. Once again, the two Nazis stood and made sure all their documents were signed and stowed, and then excused themselves. The two made their way through the door and closed it behind them.

Back in the private room, Jerry Matthews said, "All tribal leader qua collectivists stink - those two can not wash the stench off themselves."

Hosea said, "Mister Matthews, true enough, but we all live in the world as it is. Would you excuse Brenda and me, and we will meet you in about ten minutes and go through the buffet line?"

The request came as no surprise to about smartest lawyer on Wall Street, Jerry Matthews. He represented those people with loved ones trapped by the Nazis and lucky enough to have the means to ransom certain ones of them out of Germany's camps.

The genius, Jerry Matthews, had already worked out that this Airline Hostess is sweet on the lovable Iberian Giant. He replied, "Of course not - take your time. I will have a cup of coffee and wait."

Once they were alone, Hosea said, "Dear Lady, I need to have the ABB project's departure to New York, and all the paperwork dates delayed for two weeks."

"Damn it, Hosea! I hope there is a good reason for having to do all that work and pissing off the passenger I must bump from the flight."

Her part-time PVDE agent lover had no choice except to tell her the truth about Anna Bass. He concluded by saying, "She will arrive at the hospital soon, and the surgeon will perform the surgery, and the nurse will accompany her back here. She needs the extra two weeks to recuperate as she is seven weeks alone, but there is no pressing need to delay the father's return. Besides that, he is a businessman and needs to get back to work."

At first, anger and then sympathy swept across Brenda's face after his explanation. "Well, I sympathize with her - as I had that operation a year ago, and recuperating - both physically and emotionally - is tough. After I get the paperwork re-issued, would you introduce her to me so I can give the updated ones to her - now there is no change about her father's travel so that she will be alone? I suspect she would like nothing more than seeing a friendly female in her time of enormous foreboding as she recuperates?"

"Yes."

"By the way, Lover, who was the doctor?"

Hosea stated both the doctor and his sister's name along with the Hospital Operating Room, where he practiced.

Brenda smiled, "Great! He was the one who did my operation, a good choice! Let's join the others, and keep this secret among us two unless we absolutely must bring in Wentworth. Do you agree?"

"Agreed!"

By the way, Lover, I go to bed about 11:00. Can you come by my room for a nightcap by about ten-thirty?"

Hosea's white, straight teeth shined as he smiled with pleasure. See you then."

On Brenda's next trip to Lisbon one week later, she slept twelve hours and refreshed herself afterward. She then removed the 'Do Not Disturb' sign from her door as usual, and soon there was a knock. It was Hosea. She opened the door and grabbed him, trying to pull him to the bed. Thirty minutes later, the two spent lovers held each other. Brenda said, "I needed that!" Then she asked, "Is the ABB lady back in her room?"

"Yes, and she is alone. Anna's father told me, 'Mister Garcia, I am leaving my daughter in your hands. Thank you for watching out for her safety.' Anna is taking some meals in the buffet room. I told her, 'you and I would be seeing her this morning.' So she expects us."

Later, when Brenda and Hosea knocked on Miss Anna's room door, she opened it and welcomed Hosea and his friend into the room. Anna Bass sat on her bed, working on her Portuguese language using the traveler's phrasebook.

Hosea said, "Anna, meet Brenda Smith, who is one of my bosses for my part-time job. When I asked for the delay for you, it was she who did the paperwork necessary to change all the schedules. She wanted to meet you because she knows your doctor."

Anna looked at Brenda and said, "Oh? Oh! Brenda. I think he is a caring, wonderful man. The pain came the next day after my operation, but, "looking at the date on the ticket you brought, "I will be ready to fly for sure by that time."

Brenda said, "I like Doctor <name> and had a growth removed that might turn malignant as well. I was flying a week later - and I mean doing hard work while flying except some of my cabin crew friends stepped in to help from time to time."

Anna stood and walked around to Brenda. Each held the other's two hands, which turned into hugging each other. Finally, Anna said, "I have had a streak of excellent luck, and that happened after a streak of terrible luck. Getting out of a German camp was a stroke of golden luck. Now I have met a friend in you, Brenda, and suddenly I am glad to be alive once again."

Hosea, observing this interchange between the two ladies, had trouble restraining his tears. Since PVDE agents may not cry in public, he said to the ladies, "I will be in the coffee shop having a snack before I punch the clock? You ladies are welcome to join me later if you wish."

———

Later, Brenda and Anna were making their way across the lobby, going to have breakfast at the coffee shop. There they encountered Robert Wentworth sitting at the counter reading a report while drinking coffee. The moment he saw Brenda, he stood, and the man's face lit up, and he said, "Before you introduce me to this lady, Judy Becker [In **Hopeless Romantics Vol IV**] said a big hello to you, Brenda, and that she and her Frenchman are as much in love today as they were the first day. Who is your friend?"

Brenda introduced the two and said to Wentworth, "She is the Human Cargo who traveled to Lisbon on the project you know as ABB. She is on my upcoming flight to New York in 8 days." Extremely interested now, Robert looked at her carefully. Congratulations on wiggling out of a death trap, Anna. Maybe the three of us could talk before you fly if you would join me for dinner this evening, perhaps?"

"Well, any friend of Brenda is a friend of mine because she has gone to bat for me. How does 7:30 this evening sound, Mister Wentworth?"

They both nodded approval, and Wentworth said, "I will join you two, then, Miss Bass and Miss Smith."

Later the two ladies were sitting alone eating their breakfast and engaging mostly in girl talk. Once they finished, Anna asked, "Who exactly is Robert Wentworth."

"Well, he has been Killing Nazis when he could get away with it since 1930 - he traveled extensively in Germany selling foodstuffs to the starving people. No one even read his reports that the Nazis were rearming themselves as the world became isolationists. He and I have a close working relationship, and he was the sperm-donor of the co-worker who is my counterpart on the other flight to Lisbon each week. He was a British Navy Officer during the Great War and is now married to the woman who gave birth to my friend. A Nazi named Becker was the birth-certificate father's name and the name she carries, but her mother, an English Woman, cuckolded the Kraut and she became pregnant by Wentworth."

"Wow! What an exciting world in which all you spooks live your lives."

"Well, it is exciting and dangerous in a place like Lisbon - the death rate for we 'spooks,' as you call them, (while making marks with her fingers) is very high on all three of the sides here in Lisbon."

Anna had a puzzled look on her face and asked, "What is the third side?"

"The Stalinists, like Hitler and Tojo, are out to rape the world and convince the victims to enjoy the ordeal."

"Whew! That is heavy thinking, but... it fits the facts. But, why doesn't the Government of Portugal do something about you guys bumping each other off?"

"Heh, heh, What is in it for them? They want to keep the lights on and stay out of the shooting war, so the only time they get involved in our little sideline wars that go on here is when it might affect Portugal's neutrality."

"Hmm, That, too, makes a lot of sense."

By the time the two ladies finished their coffee, Anna said, "I think I feel well enough to walk along the beach. Mister Garcia requested that I don't do that unless he accompanies me - for security reasons, but I hate to keep interrupting his day."

"Anna, Mister Garcia is being paid very well for his services, and it is no bother. Having said that, however, meet me here at 3:00 when a friend of mine and I walk along the beach, and you may go with us - we stroll, and if you get tired, we will return to the hotel."

"Thank you, I accept."

————————

Promptly at 7:30, Anna and Brenda entered the buffet dining room and saw Robert Wentworth near the serving line sitting alone. They walked up and greeted Robert. Wentworth asked, "Would you like to fetch yourselves food and let's adjourn to one of the off rooms for privacy? Sea Bass is the fish specialty tonight, and I recommend it."

When the ladies returned with their full plates on a tray, Robert stood and led the way to the same meeting room, Brenda always used for meeting the Nazis.

The two talked small talk at first, where Anna told them about growing up in Western Rhode Island's rural area. She explained, "My ancestors' legacy was first to build whaling vessels, then fishing vessels and currently yachts and upscale sailing vessels. I lingered in Grenoble after graduating and the Germans found me. You know the rest of the story."

When the three were eating a dessert, Robert said, "Please tell us the sequence of events in the German Camp and the people involved after the commandant of the camp summoned you to his office."

Anna repeated precisely the sequence of events that happened and her transport to Berlin, and concluded with "The Gasthaus was surely rented by the Gestapo for high profile Europeans in the process of leaving Germany. We didn't talk to each other, just nodded and stayed out of each other's way."

Wentworth pulled out a photo of Hans Romberg dressed in his Gestapo uniform, and another of him dressed in his Lufthansa Pilot's uniform. "Is this the young man of the two who took you to the Gasthaus?"

"Yes, sir."

"Any unusual thing happened on the ground or during your flight here?"

"Two things that seemed strange to me. One is the flight itself. I know something about flying. My first solo happened at 15 years old and was in a mail plane. The trip to Lisbon was very rough because the pilot did not attempt to fly around the storm. I was not frightened. My thinking was that surviving the Nazis was a miracle - I barely avoided death. The probability of dying in a commercial flight as a passenger in a Condor was nearly zero - so I just relaxed and thought about how what I wanted to do with my life after I became a free person. By way of explanation, if aviation doesn't happen to be one of your specialties, the German Condor is a marvelous, dependable machine. I can not imagine why that pilot flew-by-the-book because those fat bureaucrat passengers arriving a couple of hours later wouldn't matter one way or another. If he cared, he could have gone around the storm. I would like to think he hates Nazis down deep and wanted to cause them to get airsick, but that is only my dream. I had no fear because I have studied those aircraft, and they are as close to crash-proof as an airplane can get. And there is something else."

"Oh?"

"Gestapo agents are not gentlemen. But, this person," pointing, "Is a senior airline pilot and just doesn't have the personality of a Gestapo agent."

"Go on."

"For example, after we landed, I was the last person off the airplane because the seating assignment works that way for flying Jews, I guess. As I was walking to the cabin door, I looked directly into the eyes of that Gestapo Agent, now the pilot - who had been thanking everyone for flying Lufthansa. We recognized each other at once. He also was one of the two who got me released from the Camp. He even gave me a fleeting smile of recognition, which I took as congratulations to me - and I smiled at him because I couldn't help it."

Brenda asked, "Anna, any chance you could seduce him after you spent some time to get back into excellent physical shape?" ,

"Like what kind of physical condition?"

"So that you could ski down the mountains or cross country

again?"

"I am confident I could in a few weeks - if he didn't seduce me first!" Both Wentworth and Brenda Smith laughed.

Brenda asked, "You are fluent in French, German, and what else besides English?"

"Spanish, as Hosea drills me in Spanish Diction whenever we are along talking. I also am hard at work on my Portuguese phrasebook."

The three talked at length about her private school education in Rhode Island and advanced schooling in Grenoble. Soon as she talked on and on, not only did Brenda make a new friend, so did Robert Wentworth. The master spy asked, "What do you think about working in the shadows here in Lisbon. First, Brenda needs some administrative help because she spends very little time in Lisbon. All the paperwork rescheduling your flight, for example, was time-consuming and very hard work. Being employed by us would not be the highest paying job you could find with your education and experiences."

Yes, I would do that, gladly, because if you provide my lodging and food and pay me a modest salary, I would be happy - I was an unplanned trust fund baby so money is a secondary consideration. How might such employment play out, Mister Wentworth?"

Wentworth and Brenda sat up straight because both were interested.

"We two work with both the Brits and the Americans. When you and Brenda arrive in NYC, a Latino by the name of Constance Santos of American Intelligence will meet Brenda and you at Border Control. She will interview you, send you home to recuperate from having the pre-cancerous growth removed, and interview you again in-depth later. If accepted, there will be some rather physical training - can you do that? Constance will learn that I am interested in your coming to work for us as an administrative assistant for Brenda and me and Santos will decide if she can get the funds to pay the expense of your employment. If her assessment of you is also positive, then your employment starts. Then, you will return to Lisbon, where I hope you will position yourself so that the Gestapo qua Lufthansa Senior Pilot will fall hopelessly in love with you. Santos will give you a manufactured employment record as an air carrier counter employee. Still sound like something of interest to you and do you like such a part in this war, Anna?"

Excited now, she almost jumped up and down exclaimed, "Oh Yes!"

===============================

Hans Romberg was tired because he did the preliminary clerical procedures himself on the new Project B47. He had spent most of the day in the Eichmann's office of the Gestapo District office, typing the request-for-release letter. Hans cursed to himself while two finger typing at the expressed orders of the Boss. The clerical staff sat outside Eichmann's office, laughing and doing their nails. 'Adolph Junior's' policy - which was the nickname Hans had given his Gestapo boss - was that not even one of the clerks should know what he was doing. Hans knew his next flight schedule to Lisbon and calculated all dates around that one. Once finished, he sealed and dropped the letter to the camp commandant in the outbox, checked again that the paperwork he brought from Lisbon was chained to his wrist and went home.

At home, he took out the papers and interspersed them in the topographical aerial maps describing airfields with information on each stapled to each field. He then put the navigational aid books back in the rack. The book sat between another book on the Condor, and another on emergency landing strips to use if he needed to sit the airplane down.

He was eating a bowl of stew when there was a key unlocking his front door, he had forgotten all about Frau Manfred coming over tonight. He stood, and she rushed to his arms, "Eat your damned food and take me to bed. I was with my husband twice on Sunday before I took him to the airport - he is frightened that he might freeze to death this winter. But, I thought about you while he was trying to please me and relieve his passions."

Hans smiled as he thought, "What a pig you are, lady!" and said, "Welcome, Frau Manfred, but I must clean the kitchen and then take a shower first. Want to relax with my Beethoven music while you wait?"

Once they were in the bedroom and finally getting into the position to copulate, there was a loud, pervasive knock at the front door. The two were silent, and Hans asked, "Did you see your husband board the aircraft?"

"It can not be him if his flight didn't take off; he would be home already."

Hans relaxed and went to the door in his underwear brief and asked who it was. "It's me, Adolph Eichmann."

The chains came off, and the Boss said, "Looks like I am interrupting your party - does she have a friend," grinning broadly?"

"Afraid not!"

"I am sorry to have to interrupt a sword fighter in the middle of the sport, but it's necessary. I am not going into the office in the morning, and before flying out again, I need to look at your documents and take one of them with me, of course."

"Yes, Sir. Let me break the news to the lady because she can come back tomorrow night. We were just about ready to begin partying. Heh heh. Have a seat, Herr Eichmann?"

When Frau Manfred came through the living room, Eichmann stood in deference to her. Neither gave any indication that they knew or had ever seen the other. Hans walked her to their car and said, "I am sorry, maybe you will return tomorrow night?"

"Yeah. I will see you, sweetheart, and we will talk."

Hans walked back into his apartment, and Eichmann sat reading today's newspaper. The pilot reached above the Senior Gestapo Agent's head and said, "My documents are in this book," as he pulled down a volume of maps and descriptions of airports and landing strips. Suppose ReichMinister Himmler sent you to search my apartment for incriminating documents. Want to try to find them?"

"Damn! I knew you were the right candidate because you are so cleverly security-conscious - my what presence of mind you have to think of hiding them here. He started through the book and gave up and handed the paper to Hans.

"Here they are," as he as Hans went right to them. He showed the profile and picture of the next person to be ransomed from a Camp along with a carbon of the letter written to the Camp Commandant over Eichmann's signature for the release of the next prisoner. Finally, Hans continued, "Here is the most important document to the Reich which is the original of the deposit slip signed by American Jerry Matthews and Jason Orta, the bank executive."

Hans thought, "Of course this document was why he ruined my sex-date, and the other papers were just fodder for the evil Gestapo Chief to look at and verify that I had not put Eichmann at threat. Hans looked at the man carefully and for the first time, he consciously hated him. He thought, "Eichmann suddenly looks like a circus freak! I must be cautious and not allow my loathing to show."

Eichmann said, "Well, Hans, Herr Himmler could issue an order at any time to search the contents of my office safe, but the documents are safe with you, as you have demonstrated. Please keep them, and I will only take the funds transfer slip with me. Does that seem safe enough for you? Sorry, I ruined your evening, but what we are doing is important revenue for the Reich. I am going to be very busy getting set up to move people to the East in the future, and I will just drop by on the <date> after you conduct the Lisbon meeting Project B47. You should spend your weekly half time working hours in the office, however, when specifically not working on our project. We agree there?"

"Yes, Sir."

Eichmann and Hans stood and did the Nazi salute, and then Adolph extended his hand, and reluctantly, Hans shook it.

After his visitor left, the Pilot filed the documents away and washed his hands with soap."

===============================

During the next three months, there were nine ransomed prisoners released, and all operations went according to plan. At one point, the U.S. Government even paid the ransom for one theoretical Physicist incarcerated by the Germans - that information came out during the payoff meeting process. Eichmann was busy preparing track construction schedules and ordering side tracks be built to specific points, so the entire project was now Romberg's - conducted over Eichmann's signature. Intense construction was beginning in Occupied Europe until Eichmann only had time to pick up the deposit receipt furnished by Jason Orta from his bank that Hans had hand-carried to him. They both began to think their ransoming operation was a well-ordered machine.

Going into the fourth month, today's ransomed prisoner walked off the plane. Both cockpit duo noted another Condor been prepared for tow beside theirs. Hans looked at its number and thought, "Willi, my friend, driving driving either to or from Bueno Aires is here. Now only Hans and the co-pilot were left in the plane before it would be towed to the tarmac as its next flight was in three days. They were filling out their paperwork, and the co-pilot said, "I met a woman at the Palacio bar, and I am kind of in a hurry to hold her in my arms - I don't have the luxury of visits by a traveling Wehrmacht Officer's wife the way you do, Hans. Will you finish up here and let me leave early?"

The senior pilot chuckled, "Yeah, go ahead and quickly dip your wick and relieve your passions. Maybe I will run into you guys - I would like to say that I have something working in Lisbon also, but that is not the case, so I keep looking."

"Greta's got a lot of friends, want me to fix you up?"

"No, thank you, Mark. I will continue to seek my fortune on my own."

With all the entries in the post-flight procedures finished, Hans saw a towing machine hooking to the front strut of his aircraft. He stood, verified the airplane was empty and walked down the mobile staircase. Once he entered the terminal, he began walking toward the pilot's lounge.

In the lounge, Hans found Willi Shoemaker stretched out napping. Romberg continued to the toilets and refreshed himself and then returned to the sleeping pilot friend he last saw in the Adlon Hotel bar in Berlin.

Willi, finally awoke and stretched, and then he saw Hans Romberg and smiled as he stood. "Hello, Hans, and if I hadn't already told you I like for my friends to call me Willi. Thank you for doing so. I was dreaming of a peaceful country scene where I grew up and woke to see a friendly face in a world of monsters. How great is that?"

"Hans said, " Wonderful! I have a routine I usually follow after I land, and my passengers disembark. But today, I saw your airplane being towed and decided to say hello. So here I am."

"I was just resting from a long flight because I lost an engine after I left the Azores on the Lisbon leg of my never ending trip from Argentina. This leg was on only three engines - slowly. My crew and I will stay in the Palacio Hotel/Casino tonight while the ground crews repair it. If they can not fix it, a replacement must come from Germany.

"Better that it happens here than over the ocean, good Buddy. Congratulations on not ending your life just yet! I was going out to wait for the shuttle to the Palacio, want to go together?"

Willi studied his friend's face for a long time trying to make a decision and finally said, "Since it is two of us, Let's take a taxi and voucher just half the fare each. We can tell each other something about our personal lives."

Once in the air terminal's hall walking toward the main entrance, both pilots carried a suitcase and a briefcase each. They were waved through the border control because both wore their Lufthansa badges. Outside they got into a taxi line to await their turn for a taxi.

Both pilots noticed a lady standing on the sidewalk watching the two. The two pilots stopped in their tracks. The lady was fit, well dressed, and groomed. Hans studied the woman in detail, first thinking, 'She goes to bed with some super lucky man!' Then he vaguely remembered some woman who favors her but could not bring to mind her name or where he met her. He tried not to think about her as the two moved up in line. Each movement required picking up two bags stepping forward, and putting them down.

Romberg walked behind Willi, and suddenly The Argentina airplane driver put his bags down to wait. Hans sensed that the lady was waiting for Willi, and he had been awaiting her. Hans reasoned, "I screwed up their date with each other - why in the hell did he not introduce me to the stunning lady?"

Hans kept looking at the twentyish woman whose fit body radiated total health. He swooned, "She is very much the person I wish to hold in my arms, but she is Willi's squeeze. Forget it, Hans, you must make do with the fleshy Ms. Manfred -complete with hanging biceps - when you return to Berlin. You ask too much!"

As the line inched toward the taxi-loading point, Hans sensed that Willi was making hand signals to the young lady that Hans couldn't see. Finally, they reached the loading point and the two jumped into a cab, and as it pulled away, Hans felt dizzy. He thought, "I remember her now! She was ransomed out of a German camp by Eichmann and me, and now she looks like a million Reichmarks. But that makes no sense why would Willi be courting her? Oh shit! Her father is a money bags from Rhode Island, what is she doing in Lisbon?"

Finally, Willi was tapping him on the shoulder in the back seat of the cab, "Wake up and focus, Hans, we are almost at the Palacio. Are you off in dreamland somewhere?"

"Yeah. Every time I come back to Lisbon, I refresh my awareness that somewhere in the world that are healthy people who plan to live and pursue their life. I am still paining from the fact that the Russians have bombed Berlin for the first time, and our fat Luftwaffe commander swore that would never happen. What will happen if the Americans start swinging their weight in Europe, Willi?"

"I don't think the Yanks will do that because the military government of Japan has given them other uses for their hardware and personnel resources."

"If you are wrong... Well, I don't even want to think about that."

Willi smiled and said, "Yeah. Me, either."

Once the two friends registered at the Palacio and went to their separate rooms.

Hans reasoned, "The former Prisoner must be right behind us to visit Willi! The crazy airplane driver dropped his suitcase and briefcase in his room and raced downstairs to the small off-lobby bar and ordered a beer. He sat at the counter so that at that angle, he could observe people entering the main door of the hotel lobby and note if they walked to the elevator bank.

About fifteen minutes later, the former ransomed refugee, Anna Bass, came through the door with powerful steps and purpose written all over her body. "Shit, the ex-refugee is definitely Willi's girl! How can this be? The gods are cruel!" He watched her disappear into an elevator and watched the floor indicator hand sweep, only to learn he and Willi were on the same floor, and Anna's destination was their floor.

Hans reluctantly trudged up the stairs back to his room, initially to shower and shave. He noticed a note stuffed under his door, and once again, it was from Jason Orta, the Pro-Nazi banker, about tomorrow evening's meeting. Then he thought, "I feel awful at the prospect of dealing with that piece of shit and will go to the beach alone and take a quick swim to clear my mind . The air is chilly, but the water is still warm. I am not in the mood to mingle with my crew because anything they can say, I have heard three times already."

Hans locked everything valuable in the room-safe and carried only his room key pinned to his trunks. He put the hotel's guest robe around him and grabbed a towel from the W.C.. He then walked down the stairs and out the lobby door and down to the water.

Noting the beach was virtually empty, he said outloud like a crazy man to nobody, "Damn! I have the whole ocean to myself," while laughing like a hyena at his own joke. He swam for a half hour and finally got out of the water trembling in the chilly air.

He walked over to where he had left his bathrobe, put it on, and sat on a human-made rock bench. He then picked up his towel, and vigorously rubbed his body and finally his head to dry his hair.

A familiar voice from his past coming from behind him said, "Be careful or you will pull all the hair out of your head - I heard the Reich is reluctant to promote men with bald heads."

Shocked, Hans shot to his feet, turned around to face the voice he recognized after more than three months. "Guten Tag, Anna, I know your face and voice, but I don't know your body and only remember your first name."

Anna Bass, alone now, said, "I will take that as a compliment." She stated her name and said, "For starters, my working name is Judy Wood - please remove my birth certificate name from your memory." To refresh your memory, she stated the date of her flight to Lisbon and asked, "Are you still trying to make your passengers airsick?"

Hans was at ease now and said, "Ha ha. Every chance I get if I can get away with it. What on earth are you doing in Lisbon, Judy?

"I am Brenda Smith's assistant - and that means I help her facilitate the ransoming of more of those poor creatures like I was who are in the German camps. Some refugees go to New York, Bueno Aires, and London."

"The reason I came to this deserted beach is that I called your room, and there was no answer. My conclusion was that you came here vaguely hoping to find a real live person - me. I walked down to the beach after I left your friend Willi hoping to encounter you."

"I am flattered but curious as to why you would do that. Aren't you and my friend Willi a loving couple?"

"The short answer to that is a resounding, NO. Willi is not my type and is true-blue to a woman in Argentina and, as such, has zero interest in a romantic relationship with me - and vice versa."

She didn't pursue personal talk but changed the su subject and said, "One reason I came down to the beach is to tell you that you will see me - rather than Miss Brenda Smith - in the meeting at the

Monte Estoril tomorrow night. It is important that Jason Orta, the Nazi banker, is not aware that we ever saw each other before that meeting. Another reason is that my official name is Judy Wood, so please address me in public as Judy or Miss Wood as you and I are and must remain, total strangers, when in the presence of others."

A massive relaxation came over Hans, and he trembled after he became aware of exactly who this woman is and the role she plays. He smiled warmly and said, "That makes sense, Judy. And I can act. In secondary Gymnasium, I was a dramatic performance star on-stage and always loved two things: theater and flying. With the rise of the Third Reich, I raced off to become a pilot. My triple ace status came from shooting down Russian airplanes - whose weapons often didn't work well enough to shoot back if I am fully honest. So, don't worry about my acting skills. They are right up there with my flying skills. You said two things?"

"Hans, If I showed you bank records where the ransom money you are collecting for Eichmann is not going to Germany's treasury, but to some private individual with a Bank account in Bueno Aires, would that change what is important to you as you do your part to execute this war?"

Hans was shocked. He finally answered, "It would only confirm my suspicion, but I facilitate the ransoming of those prisoners to Lisbon because what I do is the Human thing to do. I would have asked for transfer long ago, except a chance to rescue someone like you became normal for the past three months. If you were to tell me that Eichmann is the beneficiary, I might want to kill him on the spot because I would be so angry - hell! That would mean I am delivering payoff money to a global gangster."

"Working for thug is precisely what you are doing, but it's worse than that." All of a sudden, Judy grabbed him and held his body next to hers. Hans immediately held her firmly, but she backed off and said, "I see a couple walking to the water's edge, and I want them to see us doing what they would expect us to be doing."

She continued, "Hans, you are delivering money just like any thug working for a mafia in Italy. But you must keep doing it to bring out as many prisoners as possible while you can. Ransoming prisoners will end soon, however. The Germans are methodical accountants, and it is only a matter of time before this opportunity we exploit closes. Brenda thinks it will close when their number-crunchers figure out that the expense turns out to be mountainous compared to the paltry revenue they get from this ransoming project. You should be aware that those above Eichmann - if anyone - accepted the ransoming plan in the first place to earn hard currency for the Reich." Raw materials for armaments are enormously expensive, and every vendor wants payment in hard currency - as a contrary testimony to the esteem of the Reichsmark.

"You are right, Judy, and I will be fall-guy. Whether Eichmann's superiors know or if they don't know they will find out that I am the runner - and I am still a dead man."

"Maybe not - i.e., not if everyone continues the process. I will let you know when it is time to leave Germany for the final flight to Lisbon. Keep in mind that events happen quickly in intelligence circles."

Hans looked in her eyes and said, "Of course, the ransoming process won't continue once the accountants learn that Eichmann is a one-person show for personal ill-gotten gain. That means that Himmler will order me murdered at once as a cover up - my initials are on every ransoming document as signing for Eichmann." There was silence for a moment while both were thinking of consequences. The pilot continued, "So be it - several million are going to die globally as this war rages on and on until someone's surrender."

There was more silence, and Hans looked around only to find the wind from the north clearing the beach of people seeking warmth once again. Yet he wanted to continue holding this woman as she held him tighter as well.

He finally asked, "Have you and Willi now or ever have had a romantic thing for each other - by way of explanation, I saw you and him using hand signals at the airport taxi line. At that time, you only looked familiar. On the trip to the Palacio, I remembered who you are, and tested my memory to see if you would follow Willi to his room. You did."

Judy was very pleased now and said, "Well, Captain Romberg, you just might make a good spy, but the short answer is no. He is true-blue to a romantic interest in Argentina, and I talk to him during the servicing of his aircraft about matters that you do not need to know. I do know he is your friend, but please don't talk shop with him. I mean that you and he should never discuss what you do with anyone, especially not each other."

A giant feeling of relief flowed over Hans's body. He looked at her for a long time and finally said, "Anna qua Judy, I have thought about you every week at least once since you were on my flight."

She studied his face carefully, touching his cheek, and said, "I, too, have done likewise, Hans. When I was training to climb a rope, last month, my mind kept thinking about you. I know you are wondering, so before you ask, I had the fetus I carried when we met aborted, returned to my home, and made it a point to get back in physical and mental shape. I was hired and trained by the same organization that employs Brenda Smith - and then sent here to work as a Brenda's Administrative Assistant. So, here I am. That tattoo that was on my arm is now written over by one showing Aristotle with the same color of ink (while showing it to him). One last thing is that my Mom and Dad's ancestors were Rhode Island Quakers, but my boyfriend in high school was Jewish. When I applied to the College in Grenoble, I listed my religion as Jewish because of him. When the Nazis came to the party-school campus, everyone went home except we four people who listed Jewish as their religious preference on their respective college applications."

"Well," Hans said, "At this point, I am stuck on whoever you are - even if you wore the Star of David. I do hope that if religious preference question appears on a future document, you leave it blank!"

She looked at him warmly, chuckled, and said, "To be sure. In fact, if I have not read and judged you wrongly, religion for both of us is what other people in our world either believe - and practice - or believe and rebel against. In my case, I take the position that nice people often believe mystical things while I go about my business indifferent to their beliefs while they go about their business unaware that I am not like them in my fundamental views."

Hans said, "The prize goes to you for precisely reading me. One more question: where do you live now and may I visit?"

"In the less-than-elegant Granada, which is a crumbling and low rent apartment house away from the high rent district. It needs repair, but everything works. It is not too far from the Pan Am Clipper terminal. I walk or run to the beach to either of the two casinos that interest me for exercise. Also, I take the bus to the Pan Am terminal, where my work station is located. As for visiting me, not for the time being - but that will change if we will just be patient."

Yeah, I walked beside that old structure several times, seeing it without even thinking about it."

"Judy, I want to see you. What is a safe way to plan to get together?"

"Hans, I have wanted you in my body since I walked off your flight from Berlin. If you recall, I told you at the time, 'I owe you my life.' My gratitude has turned into a longing for you. The next time I will see you, however, is in the meeting with Jason Orta tomorrow night. We will plan the future for there or soon after."

==================================

The next evening, Jason Orta picked up Hans Romberg standing outside the Palacio awaiting him. The two had long stopped any attempt at making friendly small talk. The reality is that Hans suddenly hated the man but showed no emotion while Orta was indifferent to Hans . He secretly was laying the groundwork for him and his wife to live in Argentina someday. He, too, knew that the Reich's Achilles heel was the tenuous defense of it's supply lines, and that would eventually bring the Thousand Year

Reich down. They drove to the Monte Estoril in silence. Arriving at the room a quarter of an hour early, Hans jumped up on the table to do the usual search for listening devices and sat back down. Soon Jerry Matthews came in tacitly greeted the two and sat down to study documents in his briefcase.

Hosea came in escorting a new Pan Am Employee, about whom he said, "You guys, meet Judy Brown, who transferred from Pan Am's administrative offices in New York to their Lisbon office." While doing that, the PVDE Agent was passing out folders that had a copy of her employment record, complete with her picture. Miss Brown is well-trained as Brenda Smith's backup. She has administrative authority to juggle flight and seating assignments on the Clipper flights to NYC. For your information, Brenda's aircraft was delayed in New York to replace a feathered engine, so she missed this meeting."

Jerry Matthews plus the two Nazis studied the made-up employment record of Judy Brown."

Finally, Orta said to Attorney Matthews, "You are paying for this show, sir, and if you are comfortable with a substitute proctor, I am as well." Then he turned to the pilot, "Captain Romberg, Herr Eichmann said you are only the courier for his project. That means your official capacity is to cut Reich's overhead costs because you fly the airplane. Can you think of any risk this substitution poses to our operation?"

While Orta was talking, he calmly brought out a tube of sunburn lotion for his lips to indicate complete indifference to what was going on in the meeting room. Romberg remained sitting and said, "Sorry, the wind has dried my skin, but, I have no problem with this substitute, Herr Orta and Mister Matthews. I know well what it is to have engine trouble when flying. For that reason, I consider it business as usual when a substitute shows up."

"O.K.," Orta said, "Let's proceed."

After the tasks of the meeting were completed and it adjourned, again, the two Nazis left the room first.

———————

Outside the Monte Estoril walking toward the parking lot, Jason Orta said, "Damn! Brenda Smith is much better eye-candy than the new Judy Brown woman - even though the new one is younger and has a hard, fit body."

"Jason, I thought one who reached your advanced age didn't notice a fit body and mind"

"Advanced age, Hell! I do have a wife at home, but I have a girlfriend on the side. If you promise not to tell Eichmann, he and I are screwing the same Lisbon woman intermittently. She lets me know when he is in town. If Adolf knew about us he probably would be so mad until he would find another bank to do his business. Haha."

"My lips are sealed, Herr Orta. I do without a lady's company in Lisbon, but one visits me from time to time in Berlin. One night Eichmann came to my apartment to talk business while she was there. We were just getting into position when he knocked on the door. We postponed our getting it on until the next night."

"Well, you certainly couldn't tell Eichmann to take a hike and come back in an hour, could you?"

"To say the least..."

Trying not to display his boredom with this banker, he continued, "By the way, Herr Orta, I didn't exercise much today so that I will walk to the Palacio along the beach tonight - it's only about two miles."

"That works out for me because the wife delayed dinner waiting for me. Good Night, I will see you on the next case."

Hans strolled toward his hotel room, passing several people who were still milling around on the beach. Sometimes he observed lovers holding each other warmly, and the sight almost brought tears to his eyes each time. "Why can not that be me?"

The pilot finally reached the Palacio Casino/Hotel just as twilight was changing to darkness. Tired now from his spirited walk, he walked up the stairs to his room and deposited the documents in the room's locked safe.

He turned the radio dial to a local classical music station that advertised that the station was playing the complete recording of Wagner's **Tristan und Isolde** tonight. He felt light and hummed opera arias while interviews prior to and about the performance went on and on. He thought about food and then switched to thinking about holding Judy Wood this afternoon. He soon forgot his hunger. Just as the opera overture started in quiet tones, he thought, "I am not going to enjoy this four-hour opera if I don't eat some food."

At that moment there was a knock on his room door. Hans went to the door. "Who is it?"

"Room Service."

Knowing that he hadn't ordered food, he looked at the figure through the door security portal and saw a woman. He opened the door, and there stood Judy Brown. He welcomed her inside and closed the door.

She was carrying a large box of what must have been native Portuguese food. It was just out of the oven, and the spicy odor was driving the pilot crazy with hunger pains. At the same time, he was mesmerized by the sight of Judy in his room. Both froze, looking at each other, and a smile slowly formed on both of their faces.

Hans took the box from her and set it on the desk and said, "May I touch your arms again, Anna. All I remember was that yesterday afternoon they felt like steel pipes."

"Hello again, Hans, and please do."

After they held each other, the pilot's erection was painful, and she was clawing at him as well. Then she suddenly backed off and said, "Not Yet! We must have dinner and then talk. By the way, in case you are wondering, I came up in the service elevator - I know and from time to time, use the elevator code after entering the building via the truck dock. This food I bought is from a tiny diner catering to the Casino service staff locals who work in the resorts along the beach. I took a chance that spicy fish might be something you would enjoy."

Hans replied, "I definitely will enjoy it! Let's talk! You were holding me yesterday afternoon, and I learned not to feel guilt for doing so while my arms were around you - I even hoped more people would walk on that deserted beach so I wouldn't have to stop. I still want to hold you, Judy, and never let you go."

She gently pushed back from him looked in his eyes for a long time to be sure that the feeling didn't entirely come from the bio-chemicals fire-hosing inside of the man - as well as herself . "Mister Ace pilot, I ached to hold you since my arrival in Lisbon three months ago. I figured out there was something special about you because you gave me several Reichsmarks to buy food at Tempelhof, which is something a real Nazi would not do. Then, you flew through that storm rather than around it. I would like to think you did so to deliver the cargo on your Project ABB. Why did you take the standard route to Lisbon rather than go around the turbulence?"

"Ha. I told my crew, 'We have a VIP on board,' and it is imperative we get there almost on time - in truth, the reason is I knew your parent would be waiting for you with that PVDE local guard. Without thinking about it at the time, I concluded later I did it for you."

Tears were coming down Judy's face now because her emotions were so high. She said, "That was my assessment at the time - I know about flying because I soloed at 15 in a small mail craft that is a lot like the German Storch - and now I have about 250 hours of flight time. I did not fly the mail, however, but I did fly to parts vendors to make emergency pickups for my Dad's businesses."

The two stopped talking and sat on the floor and devoured the food Anna brought while remaining silent, looking at each other.

After they both had finished and refreshed themselves, Hans looked at this woman who was now the only object in this whole world he valued more than life itself."

Once they were comfortable, the new woman in his life said, "Hans, Darling, the Germans will lose this war and tyrants through history have demonstrated the reason for it (Napoleon comes to mind). Specifically, the supply lines to the Russian front are fraught with delays and no show of supplies. The Partisans in

Yugoslavia are wreaking havoc with every supply train trying to get rations, winter clothes, and armaments to the Wehrmacht. The U.S. has hired the mafia in southern Italy to report German supply aircraft flying to North Africa. British pilots interdict the lumbering cargo planes, and the supplies often never get to Romel's forces. Mussolini's police are powerless to deal with those thugs because the Mafia is on the side of whoever pays the most - and no one on the planet can get in a spending war with the U.S. That means that the thin German supply lines to North Africa hang by a thread."

"Yes, but on the other hand, the German has gung-ho zeal to fight for the Fatherland, and that counts for something!"

"No, my Love, you are wrong. Feelings for the cause are no match for an endless supply of armaments delivered where needed. For example, consider the Russians. They don't even have working toilets much less an arms industry. The U.S. is giving them artillery and fuel to fight and suffer battlefield casualties at the hands of the Nazis on behalf of the taxpayers of the U.S. who pay the bill. The bottom line is that America - and its agents - will smother Germany with military hardware falling from the sky."

Suddenly, Hans was frightened. "You are right. The Reich's push will be to acquire raw materials for armaments - which means they need more hard currency. Their auditors will figure out that Eichmann's ransoming Jews project is costing Germany net money, not earning it money."

She replied, "That is why brilliant people like Eichmann have set up naive people like you to be the fall guy, and Herr Eichmann will convincingly argue to his superiors that he didn't know what you were doing, that he just signed what you put in front of him. In the meantime, almost all of this ransom money is in Eichmann's bank accounts in South America. My take is that that Thug is well educated and an extremely brilliant man. He has already figured out that Germany will ultimately lose the war for the reasons of planning incompetence and interdicted supply trains. That Gestapo Beast, Eichmann, will in time make his escape and live on easy street in Argentina - made possible by you who will be dead. Untold millions of additional incarcerated people whose loved ones outside have no means to pay the ransom will also die."

Hans looked at this brilliant woman in front of him for a long time. He noted that as she continued to speak, the tensions in his body were gladly changing to a completely relaxed state. He finally asked, "Why would Eichmann and his bosses want to kill all those people - why not just put them to work?"

"The Reich has no resources to house and care for workers, so what else can the Nazis logically do with the Jews and misfits but ultimately slaughter them? The smart Reich Officers and Honchos are putting money aside in South America and will make their getaway masquerading as someone else. For example, some of the key shareholders of Herr Orta's bank and other banks like it are also getting rich along with the savvy Reich Officers who enjoy the the loot as will Herr Orta, for example."

Hans could not figure out what was going on in his body. He just felt sensations tingling his skin, and he looked at the lovable creature in front of him. Finally, he kissed her hand and said, "My friend Willi says that the political climate in Argentina is unstable - that their Navy supports the Allies while their Army supports the Nazis. He also says the next election could go either way and whichever way it goes, the opposition just might take to the streets to install their own man despite the voter's preferences."

"That's true. Politics in Argentina has a habit of being practiced on a powder-keg. If history is a judge, each successive regime will be worse than the previous one. The quality of the voters there are declining like everywhere else. As we speak, the thug in power there is buddy-buddy with the Axis at the moment and exports armament raw materials along with food and utility stuff and allows replenishment vessels to re-provision German U-Boats off shore. Their sitting president is so stupid until he thinks Germany can and will win the war - and underwrites the German commercial attaches throughout Argentina all the supplies they order on generous credit terms."

At that moment, Anna stopped and reached into her purse and

brought out two ledger sheet photos. One was Eichmann's account debit entries in the Nazi's account in the Lisbon bank. She gave the first document to him and asked, "Does this agree with your memory of the amounts being deposited into Eichmann's bank account? Hans was very familiar with the amounts and the dates on Orta's bank document.

She then gave the other photographic document to him and said, "This is a Bueno Aires Bank's ledger of some Spanish sounding person's name and the corresponding Credit entries in the ledger. Note that they matched the amounts and dates that the match the amounts posted on the next business day." There was silence for a long time.

Hans studied the photo of both documents and verified to Anna, "This could not be a coincidence, as fabricating this by an Allied lab is impossible - both graphic bank logo details are too detailed to be counterfeit."

Then the former star and fighter pilot, who once received a medal from Hitler himself, was hopping mad! He stood up and began banging on the furniture, but finally settled down. He asked, "How did you get these ledger sheets from both banks?"

"Hans, we have paid informants in the accounting departments of both. We pay them well to photocopy this information and pass it to us - money opens all doors and file cabinets! Moreover, the same applies to your District office of the Gestapo in Berlin."

"You sold me, Anna, as you knew you would. So, what now? My schedule is to return to Berlin in two days at 9:00 a.m. For the first time in my life since becoming a pilot, I do not look forward to flying. It occurs to me that my co-pilot does not have the left-seat hours to be qualified to make the seven-hour flight to Berlin either."

"I have a suggestion, but only after you hold me." She gave a package of condoms to Hans, and they embraced while they nervously and excitedly tried to take each other's clothes off. Their passion lasted about two hours, after which the top bed sheet was wet with their body fluids.

After both were looking at the ceiling lying beside each other, trying to catch their breath, Judy spoke again. "Thank you, Dear Hans - you have no idea how badly I needed you and our romantic exercise."

Finally, Anna got up and began putting on her clothes. Hans watched and felt the pang of desire for her again - once more before you go!" Their passions this time lasted about a half-hour.

She stood up naked again and said, "I have a busy workday tomorrow, and you do as well. Please hook up with your crew and do everything you 'sword fighters' do except take off your clothes and get in a 'fight' with another woman Heh heh. I will see you on your next trip to Lisbon."

On parting, their only two body-parts that touched were their lips. Judy was gone.

===============================

The next morning, Miss Wood was on a cloud in her apartment in the rumbling wooden structure where many of the casino service staff lived - particularly the gaming table employees and some of the wait staff and even some of the housekeeping people lived there. She put on her Pan Am administrative support uniform and caught the bus to the lobby of the Monte Estoril. She ran across the open space to the stairwell and ran up to her immediate supervisor's door, Brenda Smith and waited. Soon she was joined by Robert Wentworth about 8:30 who joined Judy to wait for Brenda.

Standing outside Brenda's door, Robert said, "Good morning, Judy. How is your new job working out for you? How did the dinner plans you had for last night work out?"

"Just wonderful, sir, on both counts!"

At that time, the room door opened, and Brenda stepped out with her suitcase in hand, ready to wait for the shuttle at 9:00 in the lobby. She said, "Good morning, Judy and Robert, I willed myself to get out of bed this morning for my less-than-exciting trip back to New York."

The three walked into the stairwell and slowly walked toward the lobby when Judy said, " I seduced the subject - his body and his brain, and heaven forbid I am in love again!" The three stopped on a stairwell. Both looked at Judy wide-eyed, and Wentworth asked, "In Love?" The three paused on a landing and began talking.

Robert Wentworth, unable to wholly accept at first all that the new hire had said, asked, "When did the feelings come alive in you and the airplane driver, Judy?"

"I first saw him face to face and fell in love when I was exiting the Condor at Portelo Airport more than three and a half months ago - and I do believe he did the same. Our lovemaking last night was one for my record-book. I made your logical arguments along with the ones I presented, on why it would be in his best interest to work for us. My explanation made complete sense to him. The clincher was that he became fighting mad at his Boss, Eichmann. The trained 'Gestapo agent' would have killed his boss in cold blood on the spot had he been there. This was after it dawned on Hans that he was just carrying ransom money for a thug, he suddenly was livid with hatred for the entire Third Reich."

Robert smiled as he knew his plan was coming together and was deep in thought. The top spy asked, "He will make his Berlin flight tomorrow as scheduled?"

"Yes, sir."

Things are moving faster than we thought and I couldn't get word to you while you two were lost in love yesterday evening. The American Spy Chief in Switzerland sent an encrypted wire. You must get word to the Medal Winner before he flies tomorrow or before the next return trip to Lisbon. That trip must be his last one. He should bring all his airplane and navigation documents as baggage with him."

Finally, Brenda spoke up and said, "It's getting close to nine o'clock, Robert, and I need to say goodbye to you two. "Good job, Miss Brown, we will talk when I get back. By the way, is every seat full on my trip West?"

She shook her head, 'Yes' and Brenda grimaced as she opened the lobby door and charged into it.

==========

Judy took a taxi to her apartment and dressed in the sexiest outfit she had. She knew that William Shoemaker (Willi) was flying in the early afternoon and she also knew she couldn't safely contact Hans again so soon after last night. Since Lisbon to Berlin today was Willi's last leg of the flight from Argentina. Wentworth's informant in the Lufthansa Repair Facility relayed that they installed and tested the overhauled engine on Willi's airplane today.

She took a taxi over to the Palacio and quickly ran up the lobby stairs to Willi's room. She pounded on the door. Willi opened the door wearing his Senior Pilots Uniform, obviously getting ready to go downstairs to board the Lufthansa Chartered Van.

Willi was pleasantly surprised at the sexy costume that Judy was wearing but said, "Come in, Judy, but I only have a minute to talk."

"You must get word to Hans in Berlin that his next flight to Lisbon must be his last. Tell him I said, 'The Nazi auditors are busier than first thought.' Tell him also to bring all his flying paraphernalia with him."

Willi repeated what she said back to her and said, "Will do. I guess there is no message about my future?"

"No. Sorry. You are right where we need you, according to Brenda and Robert."

Willi responded to a knock on his door by opening it. Willi's co-pilot, stood and impatiently blurted out," Come on, Willi, the van leaves in five minutes."

Willi and Judy were embracing each other in a passionate 'good-bye' kiss in the presence of the crew member.

The co-pilot said, "Hey, lady, Willi will be back in a week, sorry for interrupting your romantic goodbye but duty calls."

In the van, the navigator said, "Willi, you have one of the best looking Hides in Lisbon to share your bed. Lucky you! Do you have enough energy for the seven hour flight coming up?" The remainder of the crew laughed at the conquest of their Senior Pilog." The navigator said, "Hey Willi! you got lipstick on your collar."

"I will stop at the men's room at Portelo and try to wash it off."

==========

Hans had returned to his office in the Gestapo District Headquarters in the outskirts of Berlin after landing yesterday. He almost was smiling and upbeat as he walked down the hall to Eichmann's office. His mind was on his and Judy Wood's recent romantic ecstasy in his Lisbon hotel room two days ago.

On entering the outer office where the two receptionists sat, his day suddenly went to hell. Waiting for him, were two ugly, mean looking men, dressed like street thugs. The two receptionists silently sat pretending to study their paperwork in front of them. Hans just nodded and went to the door into Eichmann's inner office. Hans forced himself to be calm as he turned to the men and asked, "Were you gentlemen waiting to see me?"

They both stood and the taller one said, "Yes, Herr Romberg."

"Come right in. Would you like to have some coffee?"

Shocked, the shorter one said, "That would be nice. Thank you." One of the administrative staff jumped up and soon returned and entered the inner office with three cups of coffee.

"What may I do for you?"

The tall one said, "We are conducting a financial audit. I will say up front we have looked at your pay records and bank accounts and you live within your means so we have no interest in you. What can you tell us about your boss?"

Hans shrugged and said, "Nothing that you don't already know - Reichfuhrer Eichmann is in Vichy this week, I think, and I do some errands for him, but mostly I fly bureaucrats and dignitaries in the Storch for half of my pay. I don't ever fly Herr Eichmann anywhere. For the other half, I am a senior pilot for Lufthansa - but surely you know all of that. So what kind of information might I give you?"

For starters do you have the combination to his wall safe?"

"No. After the January meeting with Reichfurhrer Himmler and others, he had the combination changed and simply told us he will start storing things for his eyes only in the safe. I have no idea what he does for the Reich except something going on in the East, he said once at lunch."

The tall one spoke again, "One of the receptionists told us that, we had just hoped he confided the safe combination to you, secretly. We are well aware of the project he is working on and we want to find out if there are any other money trails in his safe that he forgot to report. It's a routine audit of Expenses, Herr Romberg."

"Sorry I can not help you, Gentlemen. His administrative assistants have his schedule, but he doesn't keep me informed."

Hans noticed a disappointment look in the tall one's face but said, "You are right. We were in the building auditing another project and decided to duck in here on the chance that Herr Eichmann was in town, but we shall come back next week. Thank you for cooperating with us."

After Hans and the Thugs did their 'Heil Hitler' salute they left the room. Hans was dizzy and walked over to the sink and threw up. He looked at himself in the mirror as he suddenly evaluated the wake-up call he just received from the Thugs. But, he said to himself, "Its business as usual, Hans, and you must show no difference in your attitude toward those you will be working with this week."

Later, Hans dropped the letter to the new project's Camp Commandant in a courier box stating a date and time he will come and pick up the prisoner while on his way home. He spoke to the receptionists. "Had either of you seen those or any other auditors before?"

The senior said, "Herr Romberg, I don't think they were auditors - they both needed to take a shower and change into clean clothes. But, it is a first in my five years of working here."

"Yeah, I noticed body odor as well."

On his way home later, Hans had forgotten about his visitors that day and walked into his apartment. All of his underwear was on the floor and pots and pans were out, and his living room was strewn with his aviation books. He immediately was rigid with fear. Then he felt his pocket and found the funds transfer receipt, and the new Project documents and relaxed. He knew that the thugs had found nothing.

Hans barely had time to put everything back in place when Frau Manfred knocked at his door. After greetings and she held him tightly she was crying. She blew her nose and said, "My husband remains in Russia seriously wounded with shrapnel. I am waiting to see if the Wehrmacht will airlift him home because his condition is serious. So, you and I had better take a vacation from each other until I see what the future holds, do you mind?"

"No. I certainly understand. You care for your husband and are concerned. Maybe later, we can reconnect?"

"Oh, thank you, Hans. What a marvelous man you are!"

After an uneventful next day flying the Storch, Hans Drove out to the Holding Camp two days later, Hans thought, "Hmm, I could learn to enjoy tooling around in Eichmann's BMW like a big shot, but don't get used to it, airplane-driver. This lifestyle is not you!"

The process at the camp commandant's office again happened as if Himmler himself had ordered it. The released person this time was an older man, but still very active physically and was also frightened of Hans's black suit. The man appeared under-nourished in that his clothes were too big for him. There was silence in the car driving back to Berlin.

Hans' drove away from the Gasthaus after depositing the Prisoner. He thought, "My flight to Lisbon is in three days. I must fly to Hamburg in the Storch tomorrow to take and bring back an Admiral. So, I will get the airline tickets and exit visa paperwork for the prisoner today. No matter what, I must go to the Airport Administration for the paperwork. Hmm, from there, I am going to withdraw all the Reichmark funds allowed and then drive directly to the Adlon and have dinner. I sure would like to see a civilized and friendly face, and maybe Willi will be there."

———————

Willi came up to the Adlon bar and took a seat beside Hans while the triple-ace ate dinner and sipped a large beer. The Argentina airplane driver said, "Wow! That looks good," and ordered the same. For an hour, the two talked flying, and Willi said, "I got to hand it to those engine mechanics, all four motors just purred on the trip from Lisbon today."

Hans replied, "My flight back was only about half full - I guess the bureaucrats in Lisbon want to spend a fun weekend there at the gaming tables rather than back here where the winter wind is already blowing. That means my next flight from and to Tempelhof will be full."

"And that reminds me, Mister Romberg, do you have your boss's car parked near here again?"

"Yep! I do. He is in Vichy on Reich business and left me his car again. Do you want a lift to somewhere?"

"Yeah, home. I brought only a light jacket to this bar, and I don't want to freeze my ass off in the North Wind waiting for the bus, and I live too far to hire a taxi."

The two friends' chatting lasted an hour after the waitress removed their plates. Hans finally said I got to call it a day - I was up early this morning to take a car trip on behalf of Herr Eichmann."

Just as they were about to leave, two Fraulines came up indirectly selling the chance to be intimate with them. They both begged off and stood. Each paid his bill, and they walked out.

The two drove to Willi Shoemakers' apartment complex and parked. Hans switched off the engine so Willi could finish retelling an adventure he had safely sitting his Condor down in a 90-degree crosswind at about 40 knots.

Finally, they sat in silence, Willi looked directly at Hans and shocked his friend by saying. "Judy Brown, who works for Brenda Smith and Robert Wentworth, came to my apartment this morning and told me to tell you, and I quote, 'Your next flight to Lisbon must be your last and to bring all your aircraft and flight paraphernalia with you.' Hans, my opinion of you went up several notches on learning that you were one of us. And, she wasn't running off at the mouth, it's essential for your and my health that you do as she says."

"Whew! I suspected as much as I had visiting auditors yesterday. I know now that you work for Wentworth's organization, Willi, when you are not flying. I am sorry I had to find out. But I will try not to be arrested and tortured before I leave Germany for the last time. Thank you, buddy, I will put all my flight stuff in a suitcase tonight because it flies with me. My flight is in two days, 9:00 a.m."

Willi got out of the BMW and stood at the window. He said, "Thanks for being my friend, good buddy. Good luck, and watch for bandits coming out of the sun!"

Hans was tense and nervous, driving home and gave up trying to sleep that night. Finally, he sat up in bed and thought to himself, "Hell! What you must do is no worse than a dogfight with an inferior airplane driven by an untrained pilot, relax. This ransoming has been going on for months now, and it will go on one more time smooth as silk."

Picking up the astonished but happy released person from the Gasthaus early morning went like clockwork. Hans was nervous to the point he embarrassed himself. He rationalized, "I am untrained in how to act with stealth, so I must pretend to be the fully trained Gestapo agent that I am supposed to be and show the world that I am mean to this poor Jew."

At Tempelhof Airport, the former prisoner of the Reich made his way up the stairs to the Gates and had a wide grin on his face for the very first time since the two had met in the Commandant's Office. Hans walked into the men's room while still dressed in his Gestapo 'costume' with his two suitcases in his hand. Once in a stall, he changed into his Lufthansa Senior Pilot uniform and then exited carrying his two bags. He breathed another sigh of relief because the sentry guarding the entrance to the flight line recognized and smiled at Hans as the sentry waved him through. Hans put his two suitcases on the first buggy for the baggage loaders feeling more relaxed with every step. He then walked around the aircraft to verify that there were no visible signs of a maintenance crewman having forgotten something.

Later in the cabin, he slid into the left seat as usual ready to begin the pre-flight. After the greetings, he said to his co-pilot, "Mark, how did you sleep last night?"

"Like a fallen tree, Hans. My Lisbon Squeeze loves me. This is a great day because I am going to get laid again in Lisbon tonight!"

"Well, I am afraid the lady who visits me couldn't get enough last night and kept waking me up - her husband is injured somewhere on the Russian front trying to get home on a space-available basis, so she spent the night in my bed. You up for the left seat on this flight?"

"Yes, I am ready," as they exchanged places. The copilot continued, "Aw, you poor creature worked over by a Wehrmacht Officer's wife." Even the navigator heard that and said, let's all say, 'Ahhhhhh, for poor Hans."

Romberg said to his co-pilot, seriously, we should have perfect flight weather. Would you like to take the craft up, do much of the flying, and set it down in Lisbon?"

Playfully he said, "Oh, yes, thank you! Thank you! My mother thanks you, my father thanks you..."

"The navigator chimed in jokingly and said, "Help! Let me out I would rather walk to Lisbon as everyone roared with laughter."

Now, the cabin door and the cargo bay door made a loud sound as they closed. The towing vehicle started pushing the Condor out to the tarmac. Hans had the earphones and microphone himself, and paid close attention to any communication from the tower. He fully expected a 'hold order,' but it was all business as usual. Tense as he was, Hans felt himself relaxing as he communicated with the tower and passed instructions to Mark while taxiing to the take-off point at Berlin's Tempelhof.

After what seemed like an hour waiting on pins and needles,

the tower gave the clear to take-off signal. The co-pilot lifted the fully loaded Condor into the air as if he had done it a thousand times - Hans began to ever so slightly relax as they began increasing the distance from Berlin.

Hans said, "As a safety measure, since you are flying this bird alone, I will handle all communications both to our customers and to the ground, O.K. with you?"

"Suits me just fine, and I must train myself to never take my mind off what I am doing."

Hans said while waiting, "Mark, there is no reason that after a couple more of these trips, you can not get your promotion to a senior Pilot. You have my endorsement. Today, Mark, it will be your job to tell all the passengers thanks for flying with us. I will be rushing off the airplane when the cabin door opens."

"O.K., Boss, but why?"

I will fetch my luggage from the hold and find a clean crapper in the terminal. I need a toilet that doesn't smell (I hate to use airborne crappers). Please do the Post-flight paperwork after you do the honors of thanking our guests for flying with us. I am going to go ahead and sign the form now if you promise to later fill it in correctly."

"Yes, glad too, and you do try to try to quickly relieve yourself before you dirty in your clean uniform, and get some sleep tonight, will you?"

"O.K., good buddy. Enjoy your layover in Lisbon!"

\\\
\\

After Mark parked the Condor at the gate and the cabin door opened, Hans came alive and sprinted down the stairs and to the cargo bay. He retrieved his two suitcases as the first two items to come out of the hold. He ran into the terminal clutching his two pieces of luggage. The Defector noticed that a PVDE agent who Hans normally expected was not on security duty for the newly freed prisoner on the current project. Rather, another off-duty

PVDE agent, a friend of Hosea Garcia's Hans had met was standing by an older woman and both were waiting for the slow-moving newly ransomed gentleman to make his way into the terminal. "

Over to their side, he noticed the off-duty Portugal State Policeman with whom he was friends, Hosea Garcia, standing with Judy Brown and with an Anglo whom the Lufthansa pilot didn't know but had seen once or twice in the past.

The former highly decorated triple Luftwaffe ace walked toward the three other well dressed men and Judy. Apparently they had been killing time chatting while awaiting the passengers to disembark. Garcia and the two men laughed robustly as the defector walked up to the three men plus the woman of his life, who awaited him. She said, "Hans Romberg, meet our boss, Robert Wentworth and you already know Mister Garcia and these are a couple of his off-duty friends at the PVDE."

The master spy didn't extend his hand but said, "There just might be an attempt on your life, Hans Romberg, based on a wire we intercepted from Berlin. That is the reason security is beefed up. But, welcome, Mister Romberg. Please accompany this gentleman to the men's room. He will stand guard outside while you refresh yourself and change into civilian clothes and join us in the coffee shop afterward, if you would?"

"Will do, Sir."

Once the three sat at a booth drinking with the two PVDE agents sitting by the entrance to the coffee shop, They drank tea, and Wentworth said, "Hans, thank you for joining our side. We know that you are fully on our side because you thwarted the wishes and desires of two thugs like Adolf Eichmann and banker Jerry Orta rather than share in their looting of ransom funds - you, too, could have made a bundle of money, but walked away from it. . We were really impressed that you were not trying to enrich yourself with Ransom Money. For the record and your information, we are no longer involved making those two Nazi Thugs rich . We do wish we could have ransomed more prisoners of the Reich, but the war is for the first time not going as well for Axis, and they soon would close in and shut down our project anyway - and gunned you down - for cost reasons. Our organization's ultimate goal is to kill Nazis, and our intermediate goal is to gather lots of information about Nazi abilities so that we can kill Nazis with that information. You still on board with us?"

"Yes, Sir."

He shook Romberg's hand for the first time and smiled. He said, "You will be lodging with Judy Wood, here, for the time being, per her request. You still on board with that arrangement?"

"Yes, Sir," as he and Judy squeezed each others hand.

Do you need an advance in Money?"

"No, Sir. I emptied by bank account. I plan to change my Reich-marks to Swiss francs before I leave the airport."

"Good idea. Judy will detail all of your responsibilities while we await your training in England. How is your English? Will that be a problem for you?"

Hans smiled and said, "No, sir. Throughout my primary and secondary schooling, English was my foreign language of choice."

"Judy, are you certain you want a house guest for the next several days maybe weeks?"

Judy broadly smiled and saids, "I am certain, sir."

At that point, Wentworth drank up and said, "While you guys are taking a break from getting to know each other, please drill Hans in English Diction. Finally, as both of you now know, there will be no ransom-meeting tomorrow evening, and please don't hang out where your Lufthansa peers or Herr Orta might encounter you in public. Hans, as soon as the local banker can get information about your no-show in the scheduled meeting to Eichmann, the Gestapo Thug will issue your 'Kill order' because you know too much. That means for the time being stay out of sight with Judy. Any questions?"

"I understand and agree, sir."

Wentworth stood, put on his coat, shook Hans's hand and said, "You will be hearing from me personally or someone who works for me."

==========

After the most sexually ecstatic week that both Hans and Judy could remember - and he was well known as a 'sword fighter' among the fighter pilots who strutted like peacocks back in Germany - there was a knock on Judy's apartment door. Hans was alone still in his pajamas. He fetched his luger and asked, "Who is it?"

==========

My name is Mark Spencer, and I am a recruiter for B.O.A.C. I want to talk to you about flying for us, Mister Romberg. Hans held the luger menacingly and opened the door. "Come in. But show me who you are first."

The visitor produced an appropriate badge with his picture, and Hans put the pistol back in his holster in the closet and said, "Come on in, Mister Spencer. Care for a cup of coffee? I think there is one left."

"That would be great."

Spencer said, "The scuttlebutt around the Portelo flight Ops is that you were a no show on the scheduled return trip to Berlin. You will be glad to know that your second officer flew the Condor back to Berlin without incident by taking your place. There was much bureaucratic ado in order for that to happen, but it happened."

"I can only imagine, Mister Spencer, though it is a moot point to me, as you might imagine. I am glad to see Mark get a break."

"I do hope so and say congratulations to you. In case you are wondering, Mister Robert Wentworth, a mutual friend, told me where you were hiding out. He also said that you might be available to drive one of our passenger planes. Your route assignment would be flying out of London to the neutral countries, including Lisbon. You would start in the right seat, but with a record like yours, that would be of a short duration."

"Why would you be recruiting me?"

"The bulk of our younger pilots are flying bombers and fighters now. We are desperately short of qualified people. You would be in the left seat after demonstrating your skills to one of our Instructor Pilots. We have reviewed your extensive experience with both the Storch, 109 fighters and the Condor."

"Could I be regularly given an assignment to Lisbon after the initial period?"

"Done. No one wants to fly here, and the ones who do seek reassignments - Lisbon is not a fun place for crews. So, will you talk it over with Judy Wood and tomorrow, call me your answer at this number as I am in room 331 in the Monte Estoril?"

"I will do, and thanks for the offer."

When Judy came home wearing her Pan Am office uniform, she and Hans warmly embraced. After Hans told her about his job offer, she said, "That is perfect. You will be frequenting Lisbon and will continue to contribute to the defeat of the Axis. Moreover, you may drive the airplane here or fly as a passenger space-available basis. What more can you and I ask of the gods in a time of war?"

They held each other and postponed preparations for dinner as they enjoyed the moment in each other's arms.

The End.

Appendix to VOL VII
by: Carver Wrightman

What exactly is The ENERGY PROBE, and from where did this device qua character come? Let me explain.

An uprooted storm-driven tree crashed into a speeding new 1938 Ford Coupe on an isolated, heavily wooded mountain road. A pinned and doomed Jefferson Davis Mecklenburg, the driver, lost consciousness because of the pain from his broken body and punctured organs, as his life's blood spurted.

A UFO sat down for safety reasons in the 100-plus MPH wind in the same mountain pass. The only smooth place to sit was to straddle Mecklenburg's crumpled car with the dying person inside. The Alien crew broke their standing rules of not interfering in the life or death of Homo sapiens, by wholly mending the victim's broken body as their instruments told them he was dying.

The Techies on board the UFO repaired his body, and they also supercharged his brain. Jeff now had triple the number of synapses than before. Also, they vastly and improved the cell structure all over his body to live a life of centuries. This makeover permitted Jeff to develop 24th Century Technology by the 21st Century.

But, the Aliens also implanted the idea that sharing the technology for Humans not ready for it was a disgusting thought. Moreover, it was so important to the aliens until they programmed the remade man so that he would suicide before sharing the technology.

The storm abated, and Jeff, who recently graduated from college as an engineer, walked away from the wreck. With the Second World War looming, he began his career as a Naval Weapons Consultant.

In his career since the war, Jefferson Davis Mecklenburg has been many things but currently delights in finding the partner who will make a Hopeless Romantic complete.

Carver Wrightman